C000127381

Praise For
HOLLOW

"Propulsive, claustrophobic and genuinely creepy, Hollow reads like pure nightmare fuel. I legitimately think I've got a fear of all things subterranean now."
-Robert P. Ottone, author of *The Vile Thing We Created* and the Bram Stoker Award-winning novel *The Triangle*

"Mike Salt's HOLLOW packs a dark, devastating punch that sticks with you long after you read it. My favorite work of his thus far."
-Briana Morgan, author of *The Reyes Incident*

"With HOLLOW, Salt gives us a subterranean thrill ride: a claustrophobic, white-knuckled trek into caverns and crawlspaces where the true meaning of horror and fear wait for you in the dark."
-Michael R. Goodwin, author of *Smolder*

"With his new horror thriller, Hollow, Mike Salt has created a claustrophobic labyrinth with a new set of horrors around every corner. The story wastes no time getting to the punch, and keeps up the pace as it serves up increasingly trippy situations and creative deaths as only Mike Salt can. And, with some planted easter eggs, it will delight fans of the Linkville horror series as it begins to unveil some of the series' ongoing mysteries."
-Cody Lakin author of *The Family Condition*

"Hollow is a relentless underground nightmare, in which unsettling horrors lurk around every corner. Salt drags you down to terrifying depths, leaving you to wander in the dark, fearful of what monsters might emerge from the shadows."
-Celso Hurtado, author of *Ghost Tracks*

Books By
Mike Salt

**A LINKVILLE
HORROR SERIES:**

Damned to Hell

The Valley

The House on Harlan

Hollow

PRICE MANOR:

The House that Burns

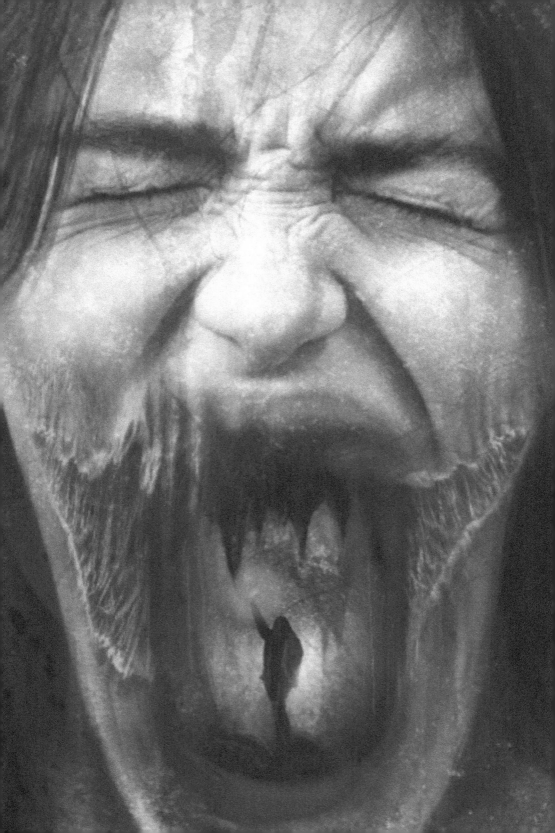

HOLLOW

A LINKVILLE HORROR SERIES

Mike Salt

DARKLIT
PRESS

Content Warning

The story that follows may contain graphic violence and gore.

Please go to the very back of the book for more detailed content warnings.

Beware of spoilers.

Contents

To that couple I ran into while exploring the Lava Beds Caves. You were so scared and lost. Your fear inspired this story. I have no idea if you actually got out, but since I never read anything in the newspapers, I assume you did.

For Great-grandpa Jasso.
I love you.

One.

Welcome to Linkville!

Tyler and Robyn read the sign as they finally arrived at their destination.It featured two bronze pelicans resting upon a bed of flowers with a stone and brick finish.

It was a nice sign.

Very *welcoming*.

Tyler couldn't remember if the sign had always been there or if it was a recent upgrade. It had been over ten years since he last came home. He didn't have any ill will towards the town; quite the opposite. Most of his memories were happy and made him wish he'd visited years sooner.

Robyn, on the other hand, didn't care to come back. She left Linkville in her early twenties without any intention of ever returning. Robyn didn't fight it when Tyler suggested a trip back home. It was only a four-hour drive for a weekend in town. Sure, she didn't exactly hide her feelings about returning (mainly how pointless it would be), but she'd packed her overnight bag and was ready to go before Tyler was even up for the day.

For the majority of their trip, the couple managed to keep up random conversation for the duration of the drive. They'd been together for over twelve years (married for four) and lived in a small town that kept to themselves. They knew everything about each other. They never had a problem talking and never needed the radio to fill dead space on road trips. They were best friends in a way that almost seemed unreal to Tyler when he thought about it. He couldn't imagine a better partner than the one that sat beside him in his truck. Yet, even with the lively conversation running at full speed, it came to a crashing halt as they passed that damn sign.

Tyler reached out for his wife's hand and she squeezed it. Maybe he shouldn't have asked for her to come? She knew Bird and was genuinely excited to see him again, but this town gave her anxiety. Maybe she was right when she suggested they pick up Bird and take him north to their place.

Tyler shook it off and squeezed her hand back. "You wanna grab something to eat before we crash at Bird's place?"

Tyler watched the idea kick around in her head for a moment before she settled on a place. "How about that steakhouse we used to go for? You think they still have a lunch menu?"

"You mean, *my* steakhouse?" Tyler said as he shot a thumb to his chest.

"Oh, yeah," Robyn said with a laugh. "I forgot it was called 'Tyler's Steakhouse'... and I also forgot that lame joke followed each time we brought it up."

"Ouch," Tyler winced, "with that attitude I don't think there will be room for you in my establishment."

"All jokes aside, I wasn't hungry until you brought up food. If you don't quickly find me some food, I *will* stab you."

Stomach full and attitude lifted, Robyn wiped her face with a napkin and shoved her plate toward her husband. There was still half a steak sandwich and some fries left for him.

Tyler picked up the sandwich and devoured it in a bite and a half.

My god, she thought as she watched the sandwich disappear with little effort.

Tyler was a bigger guy. He stood over 6' 2'' and towered over her measly 5' 4''. His hair was short, shaved close to the scalp because his hair was thinning. It worried her at first that he would have an oddly shaped head and she wouldn't know what to say to him, but luckily he looked great. Robyn had long, brown hair that she generally kept down. Her large eyes were covered with glasses most of the time. She wasn't blind without them, but they did help. A couple of months ago, the couple decided to diet and work out. They had let the winter pounds stack up over the years and decided to do something about it. Robyn fully expected to have to hold his hand through the entire process, but to her surprise he was on top of it. Meal-prepped and everything. He was motivated, too.

That was until he shoved a sandwich and a half down his throat in an impressively short amount of time.

"We good here?" Tyler said as he brought a beer bottle to his mouth and washed down the sandwich.

Robyn opened her wallet, pulled out several dollars, and placed them onto the table. "Yeah, let's get rolling."

Back in the truck, Robyn ran her fingers through her hair. It was a nervous tic she picked up sometime ago. She usually noticed she was doing it while the couple were snuggling on the couch watching a horror movie. Robyn loved a good horror movie to finish a long day, but it didn't stop her from getting anxious while a stupid college student was chased down with an ax.

Why was she nervous?

It wasn't like she was going to visit her family. Her annoying niece and her husband (along with a million kids) had no idea they were even in town. Her sister was too wrapped up in her own world to notice they were in town. Robyn didn't have to worry about running into anyone. The biggest chance of an accidental encounter was at the steakhouse, which was already behind them. Now they were going to meet up with Bird, and that was something she was really looking forward to.

Bird was a good kid. His real name was Tyler, but seeing how that was her husband's name, they nicknamed him T-Bird, which eventually evolved to Bird. He was taller than Robyn, probably just under six feet, and scrawny. Like a walking skeleton.

Bird had left Linkville the same summer ast Robyn and Tyler. He went south and landed in San Francisco for art school. After graduating, he took a job at a marketing firm that created graphics for anything, from movie posters to magazine ads. Since Tyler recently accepted a job in Portland and would be heading north for the first time in a decade, he decided to spend a week home catching up with his family.

He let Tyler know once the plans were concrete. He offered to let them crash with him and catch up for a couple days. Easy enough. No need to be nervous. They were going to play board games, video games, drink beer, and barbecue. It was going to be fine.

So, why couldn't she shake her anxiety?

Her husband's voice snapped her back to reality. "You alright there, doll?"

"Yeah, I'm fine," she said, forcing a smile. "Just ready to kick

your ass at a board game."

"Depends on what we're playin', don't ya think?" Tyler said as he smirked back at her.

"Honey, we could be playing tic-tac-toe, and I'd still whoop that ass."

Robyn turned towards the window and watched as they passed through familiar territory. Things were just as they left them. As if Linkville was stuck in a loop. Doomed to never really grow or adapt to the changing world.

They turned down Harlan Drive where a strange murder took place while Robyn was in high school. The house was still standing, its yellow paint faded and peeling from decades' worth of neglect. The back window was boarded up crudely, just as she remembered it. The house needed to be demolished. Not only was it an eyesore, but the property held a grisly and haunted history.

A couple more turns and there, tucked away down a poorly maintained road, was their final stop. Bird was spending the week at his brother's house. The place was nothing to brag about. His brother lived in a small single-wide off their parents' property. Still, Corey and his wife, Hali, were nice people, and both Robyn and Tyler really enjoyed them.

"Here we are," Tyler said as they pulled in.

At the end of the driveway, parked beside the single-wide, was Bird's orange Honda Element. Bird rushed from the front door with a backpack, tossing it inside the passenger seat as the couple neared. He nodded his head and acknowledged their arrival, but moved back inside. He looked panicked.

"What are we showing up to?" Robyn asked as Tyler parked the car.

"I don't know, he seems up in arms about something," Tyler said as he unbuckled. "Maybe he and Core got in a fight or somethin'."

The couple left the truck and walked towards the little orange SUV that reminded Robyn of a bug, intercepting Bird as he rushed towards his car.

"Hey, stranger," she said as she reached her arm out for a hug. She wasn't a *huggy* person, but she made a few exceptions.

"Hey," Bird said, almost rushed. He dropped a second bag by his feet and gave her a hug.

Robyn could see sweat rolling from Bird's long hair. His face was thinner than it used to be, but not in a sickly way. A beard had found its way to his chin and neck. It wasn't too thick, but it wasn't a day's worth of growth either. Though his arms had always been thin before, they now had some definition. When he hugged Robyn, she was surprised by the new muscles pressing against her.

"Slow down there, man," Tyler said as he walked up and threw his arms around the two of them. "You ready to leave already? Heading to Portland before we've even hung out?"

"No," Bird said as he released them and picked up his bag. He walked over to his car and tossed it into the trunk.

"Good," Tyler said. "Would be kind of a dick move to invite us down here only to then abandon us the second we arrived." Tyler threw on a smile to make sure the guilt landed; Robyn had seen that move a million times before.

"Sorry," Bird said as he turned around and walked towards the driver-side door. "I gotta go, something came up. You are welcome to hang out until I get back. I'd explain more, but I'm in a hurry."

Robyn managed to lock eyes with her husband. She could see the disappointment written on his face.

"Maybe we could tag along?" she suggested, stepping forward and locking her arm around her husband's.

Bird stopped, considered it, and said, "Sure, I don't think it would be that big of a problem... as long as you guys are down for it?"

Tyler moved to the passenger door and climbed in, Robyn sat behind him in the back row. "Where we going?"

Bird adjusted the bags and moved them beside Robyn. "To the tunnels."

The Linkville Tunnels.

During WW2, the town was nervous the Air Force base outside of town would leave them vulnerable if the Japanese were to ever attack. Their solution was to construct a bomb shelter beneath Main Street. It ran the entirety of the east side, roughly two hundred yards, all the way to Link River. Each store on that side of Main Street had access to the tunnel. The plan was to get as many people as possible into the tunnel if there was ever a need to. Since the Japanese never attacked, the tunnels were eventually cemented shut in certain areas. During the '60s, a string of break-ins and robberies were attempted using the easy access of the tunnels. It wasn't until the early 2000s that the city came together with several of the businesses and decided that they should be reopened for historic purposes. The tunnels were insanely popular with young couples looking to hang out for a while. Teenagers found the walks equally creepy and exciting. Eventually, the city stopped caring about the tunnels, so the homeless began using them instead. Soon enough, there was graffiti lining the walls and trash littering the floor. It never smelled better than the combined odor of mildew and piss.

"Why are we going into the tunnels? You gonna bring a hot date down there for some frenchin'?" Tyler joked as they carved their way down the road.

"No," Bird said with his eyes forward, focused on the road. "My brother and his wife went down there with some friends. They told Corey they wanted to show him something *interesting* and it would be worth it," he said. "That was a couple days ago, and since then they have both missed work and haven't come home. I was supposed to go with them, but I had just pulled up and was too exhausted. Told 'em I'd stay behind."

Robyn leaned her head forward between the boys. "Have you called the authorities?"

"Yeah, they said they would look into it. Got a call this morning saying they found their car but no sign of the group. My mom checked it out, but she's a little too frail to enter the tunnel. She asked me to go instead."

Robyn looked at the backpack beside her. "Why the luggage?" She caught his glance in the rearview mirror.

"I've already gone down the tunnel. And I found something."

"Wait, what did you find?" Tyler asked.

"I found a hole. It's probably only a couple feet wide. I told one of the officers about it, but I just got a call back saying they investigated it already and weren't too concerned my brother and them disappeared through it."

"And you are?" Robyn asked.

"I've packed a bag, haven't I?"

"I can see that," Robyn said. "What's the plan?"

"Something about the hole doesn't feel right. I can't really describe it, but I bet you'll feel it, too. I think that was the *thing* his friends were wanting to show him," Bird explained.

Silence swallowed the group as they drove towards the entrance to the tunnel.

Two.

The tunnel smelled just like Tyler remembered. Piss and garbage. The floor of the tunnel was damp with a layer of what Tyler could only hope was water.

They entered through the Link River entrance, which opened into the gravel parking lot where Corey's car had been discovered. The parking lot led to a neatly manicured series of concrete stairs that flowed towards the entrance of the tunnel. The trimmed bushes and meticulously kept flower beds led straight to a giant brick wall. The brick wall was tucked along a hillside, hiding the tunnel beneath it.

Everything there was lying to you.

Everything suggested the inside of the tunnel would be just as wonderful as the outside. And maybe it had been when the tunnels were first opened all those years ago. Maybe it could be again some day if a committee ever took it upon themselves to polish the interior as they had the parking lot.

Until then, the tunnels would remain dampy and pissy, unloved and neglected.

Tyler held his wife's hand as they followed closely behind their friend. Bird seemed rattled by the situation, not that Tyler could really blame him. He had no idea how it felt to have a loved one disappear. Was *disappearing* the right way to say it? What the police wanted Bird and his family to accept really didn't make much sense. "They will turn up. They aren't really missing. They are just off doing their own thing. Give it a couple of days."

But they didn't know Corey.

Corey worked his ass off. He was the type of person that was always proud of the work he put in and would never miss work without calling in first. He never experimented with drugs, so it was highly unlikely that he and Hali just slipped off for a drug-binge weekend.

Tyler could see it. He didn't even have to squint his eyes for it to make sense in front of him. Something weird had happened.

"Keep up," Bird said as they rounded the only corner of the tunnel.

From here it was two hundred yards of straight line. The walls were over eight feet tall and rounded. The original lighting source was still up and running, giving the tunnel a soft golden glow. Graffiti and garbage lined the entrance, but about three-quarters of the way down it stopped. That was the first entrance to a downtown business. The tunnel had eight entrances on the last stretch, and Tyler remembered it smelled less like piss the further in you got.

Bird came to a stop and said, "Here we are."

Tyler and Robyn encircled him to inspect the small hole in front of them.

"What are we looking at?" Tyler asked. The hole was so small he wasn't sure a person could even fit inside it. It was well hidden, between two of the old-school lights, tucked away in a dark shadow of the tunnel. Right where the wall met the ground, there was the black hole.

Bird removed his pack from his shoulder and unzipped it, pulling out a flashlight. "This is where they went."

"What makes you think that?" Robyn asked.

Bird pointed the beam of his flashlight into the hole, where it bounced off a wall of rocks several feet away before diving beneath the tunnel. "Three reasons: Because when I was walking through the tunnel and found the hole, I only spotted it because a beam of light shined from inside there. Someone was down there."

"As weird as that is, and unlikely as it is," Tyler said, "Could have been one of the many homeless that live down here. Maybe one of them doesn't like getting kicked out every night and found a way to be here permanently."

"Two," Bird continued, "I found this right where you are standing." Bird dug into his jacket pocket and pulled out a pair of glasses. He unfolded them and handed the glasses over to Tyler.

Tyler stared at the bottle-sized glasses. "These are Core's. Did you tell the police?"

Bird took the glasses back. "Yeah, they said it was only proof that he had been in the tunnel, not proof that he went down into the hole."

"That's ridiculous. That would at least warrant taking a look."

"Exactly!" Bird said as he took his backpack and shoved it into the hole. The backpack was a tight fit through the opening, but as soon as it had squeezed through, the pack dropped heavily as if full of rocks.

"What's the third reason?" Robyn asked.

Bird got to his knees and started to maneuver his body into the hole, feet first. He squeezed his shoulders through the small opening and eventually popped through. Bird braced himself and looked back at the couple. He held out his flashlight and pointed it at the wall behind them.

Tyler followed the beam as it illuminated a piece of graffiti that he would have otherwise overlooked. It was older than most of the scribbles on the wall, barely visible. More recent paintings had overlapped the majority of what was left, but the part that stuck out was obvious.

An invitation.

Painted was a picture of a mouth of a cave, with stalagmite and all. Written inside the dark mouth, in almost invisibly small letters, were the words: *For those who seek the light. Beware.*

It was a tight squeeze, especially for her husband.

The entrance to the hole was barely big enough for a large backpack to squeeze through, and her husband had unnecessarily large shoulders. The kind that would come in handy if he was a linebacker for the 49ers, but not so much working at a fish hatchery.

After he forced his way in, Robyn felt her anxiety rise again. It wasn't too late. She didn't have to go in with them, Bird made that very clear. Something inside her told her that she wasn't going to be left behind. That she wasn't going to let her fears and anxiety have her miss out on something so different from her day-to-day life. Not only to help Bird (although that was very important), but to prove to herself that she could do it.

Robyn now regretted that notion.

Why the fuck am I in here? she thought to herself as she slowly climbed down the hole, below the tunnel. The drop-off was almost completely vertical, for as far as Robyn could see. She had to brace herself with her forearms and legs wedged out against the rocks and dirt to keep from falling on top of the men.

Sometimes that was easier said than done as the walls to the hole kept getting wider. Soon enough, Robyn was spread out as far as she could. Her anxiety was palpable as one of her feet slipped out beneath her. Rocks and dust shot down below and alerted the men of the situation at hand.

Robyn heard her husband beneath her say, "Babe?"

She wanted to answer, but she was focusing her effort on not falling and sliding down the hole.

"Babe, hold on," he said.

Robyn felt her husband's beefy hands putting pressure against her dangling foot.

"Rest. When you are ready, we can keep moving," he said.

Robyn smiled down, although she couldn't see him she felt like he could see her. She leaned against the wall and tried to catch her breath. After a couple moments she removed her foot from her husband's grasp and planted it against a rock. "Okay, let's go."

Slowly, the group moved down the hole.

The rocks and rubble rubbed against Robyn's forearms, scratching her bare skin and leaving it raw. Each step down was careful and calculated. She didn't want to risk another disastrous fall.

Finally, Robyn heard what she had been waiting for since they entered the hole: "We are almost done."

She smiled as the words hit her ears. Her eyes watered and she felt her heart beat faster than when she slipped. *Almost done, we are almost done.*

Robyn felt her husband's hand grab her feet and guide her. His hands slid up to her waist as she was carefully set to the ground.

"See, it wasn't *that* bad," he said with a smile.

Robyn gauged the situation.

Where were they?

She looked up to see if the entrance was in sight. There was nothing but a long black hole that appeared endless. Her gaze moved to her surroundings. The small area at the base of the hole was barely big enough for the three of them to stand upright. She noticed that her husband was hunched over with the top of his head kissing the ceiling.

"Where to now?" she asked.

Bird scuffled around the small area and pointed his flashlight back to where he was standing.

The light shone upon a small opening, no larger than the entrance to the hole, "We keep moving."

"That's a joke, right?" Tyler said as he tried to crank his neck to get a better view of the hole.

"Nope," Bird announced as he got to his knees and began to scope out the entrance.

"B, this is nuts," Tyler said as he looked from his friend to his wife. "Right?"

Robyn looked worried. To be perfectly honest, Tyler was positive that she had the same look the entire trip down the hole, only he wasn't able to see her face in the first place. She was strong. Stronger than most people in his life, but even so, she would have a tipping point. Tyler was worried when and where that would be.

"It's not," Bird said as he stood. "I told you guys that you didn't have to come. If you want, I can carry on by myself. No harm, no foul."

"How would we even get out?" Robyn asked. Tyler looked at her as she pointed her flashlight back up into the hole.

Bird sighed. "Well, it won't be easy, but we are going to have to climb out."

Robyn shook her head in disbelief.

Tyler turned to her. "Honey, maybe we should just leave?" he whispered. "This isn't for us, you know?"

"What was that?!" Robyn screamed as she pushed her hand past her husband to point towards the hole.

Both the men shot around, trying to follow her finger.

"What?" Tyler reacted.

"In the hole, I saw a light," Robyn said. "I think it was another flashlight!"

"Are you sure?" Tyler asked.

Bird was already back on the ground, trying to spy the same light that Robyn had glimpsed.

"Pretty sure," Robyn said softly. "I don't know what else it could've been."

"I told you," Bird said as he got to his knees, "*I told you* I saw a light earlier. They are down here." Bird paused before continuing, "Listen, come with me or go, that's up to you. I wouldn't mind some help, in case they are injured or something, but I understand if you guys need to go."

With that he pushed his pack through the hole and crawled in after it.

Tyler waited until his friend was completely gone inside the dark hole. "What do you think?" he asked his wife, placing a hand on her shoulder.

Robyn turned to him and cracked a smile, planting a kiss on his

cheek. She dropped to her knees and crawled in the hole.

Fuck.

Bird pushed the bag in front of him a couple inches at a time, then used his fingers to grasp the walls of the hole and crawl forward.

Inch by inch.

Maybe I should have left the bag behind, he thought as the group talked at the bottom of the drop. However, once Robyn saw what Bird presumed was the same light, he knew he couldn't take a chance of leaving it behind and needing it later. The bag had water bottles, a first-aid kit, some smaller spare flashlights, batteries, and jerky. The bag that Tyler was carrying had similar items, but also matches, a notebook, and a silver, thermal emergency blanket.

The hole was too tight to turn and see Robyn or Tyler, but he could hear them behind him. Bird worried about his giant friend following him through the hole; for Christ's sake, Bird could barely fit through the tight squeeze, so how was Tyler fairing?

"You guys doing alright?" Bird asked.

The sounds behind him stopped as he awaited their response.

"This fucking sucks," Tyler said with a sigh. "Do you see anything ahead of us?"

Bird looked forward and tried his best to see over his backpack to hopefully glimpse the tunnel ahead, but it was no use. The backpack was taking up the majority of the hole.

"We just have to keep pushing."

Would Corey really have come down into this tunnel? Shimmy down the hole, maybe, but then decide to continue and crawl through here? Bird tried to rack his brain for a reason that would have been good enough for Corey and his group to push through. What would have given them the idea that this hole would lead them to anything worth the effort? Bird wasn't sure there was anything that could justify this trip for them . He was personally driven by the need to find his brother and his sister-in-law.

The hole began to incline. Bird felt the room between the floor and ceiling narrow. He shoved past it the incline and kicked with his feet to push through. It was tight enough that he felt a large rock slide down his spine as he passed through.

Once he'd made it, he gasped for air and thought, *That was close*.

Bird continued forward, his fingers grasping for the rocks in front of him as he crawled inch by inch. The incline was shockingly steep. He now needed to use his feet for bracing against the wall as he tried sliding backwards.

What was that? Bird thought as he paused in place.

He listened.

The hollowness of the small hole echoed every sound around him with an unexpected intensity. The scratching and scraping of his friends behind him, their heavy breathing… it was all magnified until it suddenly stopped.

Everything, all at once, was silenced.

The echoes were replaced with an emptiness that was sudden and sharp. A ringing filled the void as his brain tried to make sense of the radical change. The ringing was loud and violent. Then, through the ringing, he heard something new.

Something was hidden deep inside the hole with them.

A voice.

A female voice.

Bird listened until he was able to pick up at least one word, just as the ringing faded as quickly as it'd arrived.

Bird could hear the voice now, he was sure. It wasn't Robyn. This voice was higher than hers, more mousey.

Someone was ahead of them.

Screaming, "Hurry."

"What's he doing?" Tyler asked at the base of the incline.

"I don't know, he stopped moving," Robyn replied. "B! B! What's going on?"

Nothing.

"B! Answer me!" Robyn yelled again.

"How far up is he?" Tyler asked. He was trying not to panic, but he couldn't fully expand his lungs. The hole was hardly big enough for him to slide through. He moved at a snail's pace compared to the other two. Their small frames allowed them to wiggle through, while Tyler had to almost force his way at times.

"Fifteen, maybe twenty feet ahead?" Robyn answered.

"Okay, are you okay to crawl up there and see if he is alright?" Tyler asked.

Robyn began her crawl without answering.

Tyler waited at the base of the incline, watching his wife disappear up the hole. He tried to adjust the flashlight, but he couldn't move his body enough to find the necessary angle.

Finally, Robyn answered him.

"He is fine, says that he heard a woman's voice ahead," Robyn explained.

"Maybe it was Hali?" Tyler yelled.

There was silence as the two of them discussed the possibility.

"He doesn't know," she said. "We are going to keep pushing forward."

Tyler took a deep breath. He felt the rocks push back against his chest.

He was going to have to take shallow breaths if he was going to make it any further. The last thing he wanted to do was get stuck halfway through the hole, blocking anyone from coming through if there were an emergency.

Tyler wiggled his body until he found a section of the tunnel that would allow him to shift his body to an angle appropriate for pushing himself further up the incline. As he crawled, he felt the walls slowly tightening. Every inch he slid, he had less and less room. His back rubbed roughly against the rock and hard earth, opposed to his chest, which was flattened painfully against sharp stone.

No doubt in his mind, if he made it out of here, he would be covered in scratches and bruises.

Tyler reached forward in search of a form of leverage along the walls. He located a small rock jutting out from the rest. Tyler took hold of it and pulled himself forward. It was going to take him all day at this rate. He couldn't even hear Bird or Robyn ahead of him. Just the shuffling of his own mission. The scratching of his sweatshirt against rock and whatever else was protruding from the walls.

Another arm forward, gripping and pulling. A large rock glided across his spine, pinning his body even closer to the floor than it was previously. Tyler grunted and tried to better his grip. He strained to pull himself forward, but without gain.

In an instant, the walls seemed tighter around him. He couldn't move because his body was equally jammed. It was as if he were in a coffin, six feet beneath the earth. Alive and waiting to die.

His breath quickened painfully as the rocky surface against his chest stabbed into him. Suddenly, he couldn't move his elbows either. They had somehow managed to get stuck along with the rest of him. Tyler tried to reposition his legs in hope that he could then find leverage to push outward with his feet.

But his knees couldn't move.

Don't panic, you moron, he told himself. *That'll only make things worse.*

CRUNK!

Tyler felt the wall above his head drop. Dirt and small pebbles clouded his vision and stung his eyes.

"What the fuck?!" he gasped in surprise. "No, don't collapse on me."

CRUNK!

He heard the sound again. This time there was extra pressure applied against his spine.

CA-CRUNK! CRUNK!

The walls pushed in on both sides, his shoulders pinned as if the tunnel were giving him an unwelcome bear hug.

"No, no, no, no…"

Tyler kicked his leg with all his strength. It pushed out of its hold and found the wall. He could feel it at the toe of his shoe. There was a rock there big enough for him to step off.

With everything he had, he used his grip above to pull himself up while pushing off with his toes.

Dirt rained from above his head, thick like fog. The walls closed in on him further, forcing his shoulder to pop.

The pain motivated him enough to summon strength he didn't know he had to free himself. He burst out of the jam like the cork of a champagne bottle.

Tyler kicked and clawed as fast as he could, desperate to reach the end of the tunnel.

Behind him, down the tunnel, he heard a sound that sent chills down his spine. He shifted himself up a gear and crawled ever faster.

Hopefully, the sound had just been in his head.

But Tyler could have sworn he heard a giggle behind him.

Hopefully, he'd imagined it.

Robyn reached out for Bird's hand. She hadn't realized the tunnel had ended. It wasn't until she saw his hand almost in her face that it dawned on her they had made it through to the other side.

With Bird's help, she slid out from the hole. A couple swipes against her stomach and pants to knock away the dust and dirt as she waited for her giant of a husband to squeeze through behind her.

She suddenly had the mental image of Tyler finally arriving, only to be stuck like Winnie the Pooh. She chuckled at the idea of him squirming to get free.

SNAP!

A glow of green lit up the room. Robyn turned around to see Bird snapping glow sticks. He popped another one and handed it to her. She shook it until it was illuminated to its max.

"How far behind you was he?" Bird asked.

Robyn didn't answer. Instead, she got down to her knees and peered into the hole, trying to angle her glowstick to illuminate the small tunnel. She hoped to see Tyler army crawling his way towards her.

He had to be down there.

There wasn't anywhere else for him to get lost. The tunnel was a straight line. However, if there was a way to get lost, Tyler would be the one to find it.

"Maybe we just can't see him yet?" Bird asked.

Robyn gauged the angle of the tunnel and tossed the glow-stick down the hole. It flew down the hole and bounced for what felt like eternity. The incline was more severe than either of them realized.

Eventually it came to a rest.

It was hard to know for certain, but it was possibly as deep as thirty feet into the hole. Still, there was no sign of Tyler.

Robyn sat and waited.

And waited.

She didn't even notice when Bird sat beside her.

The green light of the glow stick set an eerie mood. It reflected off the rocks and dirt, making her feel like she was in a nightmare.

Maybe she was? It definitely wasn't what they were hoping to be doing right now. They should have been halfway drunk playing Catan by now. Robyn would have already created an empire, forcing the boys to form an alliance in order to stop her. It would have been useless. She smiled at the thought. The fictional version of themselves having fun away from *whatever this was*?

"Babe?!"

Robyn snapped out of it. She leaned in close to the hole and screamed, "Tyler!"

"Babe! How far away am I?" her husband yelled. He didn't sound very far away anymore.

"I still can't see you. Can you see the green glow stick I threw?" she screamed with into the hole with her hands cupped before her face

There was a pause that took entirely too long before Tyler replied, "No. Everything is black."

Robyn looked over to Bird to ask him if one of them should climb in after him.

However, Bird wasn't looking towards the hole. Instead, he was looking off to the right.

"What?" she said softly.

"He doesn't sound like he is right in front of us to me."

"What do you mean?"

Bird scooted closer to the hole and cupped his mouth with both hands. "Tyler!"

He turned his ear and listened down the hole.

Robyn followed.

"You guys still there?" Tyler yelled. To Robyn's surprise, his voice sounded from her right instead of ahead of her.

Bird stood and reached out to help Robyn to her feet. "Come on."

With a glow stick in hand, he waved it up and down to fully see in front of them. They moved slowly. Not only for safety, but because they were looking for the origin of Tyler's voice.

"Tyler! Talk to us!" Bird yelled into the emptiness ahead of them.

For the first time, Robyn realized how big the room must have been. The sound was swallowed and the expected echoes were absent. It was as if they were screaming across an open field.

"Ok!" Tyler answered. "This! Fucking! Sucks!" Each word was given its own time to shine. They were drawn out and dramatic. They stank of somebody that was both annoyed and slightly scared.

"Over here," Bird said as he guided Robyn over a pile of large rocks that leaned against the wall of the cavern. Bird climbed off the large rock first and once he was steady on the floor, he reached out and helped Robyn down, too.

"I! Hate! This!" Tyler continued.

Bird was right–Robyn could hear her husband so much clearer now. Wherever he was screaming from, he was close.

With a glow stick in hand, Bird investigated the wall. He waved the light slowly up and down, until he found a hole roughly the same shape and size as the one they had just crawled through.

"Babe?" Robyn yelled.

Almost immediately, her husband responded. "Ow! Fuck! Don't do that again!"

Bird pointed the glow stick into the hole. There, he saw Tyler.

Less than six feet from them.

Robyn felt her heart pick up again. Her anxiety was beginning to jump. She didn't know why. Maybe it was because she didn't realize how close they were from being separated? That she could have lost him down here? That she was afraid for his safety?

The moment Tyler pulled his ogre-like body out of the hole, Robyn wrapped her arms around him.

"Whoa, there," Tyler said as he caught his wife.

Robyn buried her face into his chest and fought to hold back tears.

"Happy to see you again, asshole," Bird said.

Robyn released herself from her husband and pushed a stray tear from her cheek.

"What happened?" Tyler asked as he brushed dirt from his pants and belly.

Robyn looked at Bird, his expression matching her own.

Confusion.

Bird shook his head and said, "I have no idea."

"We were waiting for you over at the exit we came out of," Robyn clarified.

"What do you mean? This isn't where you guys came out of?" Tyler asked, pointing back at the hole.

Robyn shook her head.

"We came out over there, about twenty feet over this boulder," Bird said, pointing to his left.

Tyler looked towards the boulder and back to his own hole. "How did that happen? Was there a fork or something that I accidently took without realizing?"

"Doubt it," Bird said. "I really doubt all three of us would not notice something like that. There wasn't a moment that I wasn't feeling every inch of that tunnel."

"Then what happened?" Robyn asked. She didn't mean to ask it, although she knew that they were all thinking the same thing.

There was a part of her that knew the answer… she just didn't want to hear it.

Over the boulder and back to where Bird and Robyn exited the tunnel, the group reformed. Bird asked for his backpack from Tyler. He opened it and pulled out two Maglites and two smaller flashlights.

"Sorry, I would have packed another Maglite if I had known at the time you guys were coming," Bird said as he handed both Maglites and flashlights out, one in each hand.

"You go ahead," Tyler said to his wife, letting her grab the superior flashlight.

Bird turned his flashlight on and examined their environment.

"Whoa."

There was another strong beam, followed by a less impressive beam, as Robyn and Tyler followed his lead.

"What the fuck?" Tyler said. His voice was monotone, as if all character had been swallowed from it by what he was witnessing.

Bird swung his flashlight around, trying to take it all in.

They found themselves in a cavern of tremendous proportions. Their beams of light bounced off the walls that were hundreds of yards away. The walls climbed high above them, doming in a field of stalactites that hung like dirty icicles. Bird guessed that if he were to huck a rock in the air, he wouldn't reach any of them. Ahead of the group, the ground was littered with stalagmites. Some of these towered over them, whereas others were only waist-high. With the powerful beam of his flashlight, Bird was able to spot a small pool of water in the middle of the cavern.

"Where the fuck are we?" Robyn asked.

"This doesn't make any sense," Bird said. He pushed his beanie from his head and ran his fingers through his hair.

"It's insane," Tyler said as his dinky flashlight fought to compete with the others.

"No, I mean this *literally* doesn't make any sense."

Robyn turned to Bird. "Elaborate."

Bird could see the look in her eyes. He was scaring her. He didn't want that. Not only did he not want to scare his best friend's wife, but it was dangerous. If she became a liability out here, someone could get hurt.

He thought about his answer and formed the words carefully. "I mean… this can't be here."

Tyler turned to him. "Why not?"

"The tunnels run down main street, right?" Bird started.

They both nodded.

"So, we go into the hole inside the tunnel, it drops us… I don't know, a hundred or so feet. Then we go down the hole and crawl probably another hundred feet before the incline. That incline, it was steeper than we thought. It probably brought us back to the same level as before, if not above the original tunnel where we started."

Bird could see they weren't getting it.

"This cavern is probably where Main Street is. Like, where that shitty-ass pizzeria is. There is no way it should be here."

Bird watched as the information clicked with Tyler. His eyes grew wide. His mouth popped open and stayed open, only slightly.

"Dude," Robyn said.

"Dude, exactly," Bird said.

He picked up his backpack and tossed it over his shoulder as he headed into the field of stalagmites in the direction of the pool of water.

Bird didn't like what was happening. However, that didn't change the fact that he needed to find his brother. And the only way to do that was to push forward.

Tyler grabbed his wife's hand as they approached the small pool of water in the center of the cavern. If it wasn't for the insane circumstances they found themselves in, this would have been a romantic location. He could see himself pulling Robyn in close and holding her within his arms. She'd grab his arm and squeeze, letting him know that she was in the moment, too. They'd stand there and take in this truly terrifying, yet gorgeous setting.

But that wasn't the way it was going to go, so Tyler tried snapping himself back to reality. Daydreaming wasn't going to help them.

Instead, they all waved their individual flashlights, looking for their next move. Their beams of light bounced off the water like rocks skipping across a lake. Behind them was a towering formation. It rose into the sky and embedded itself into the roof, like a support beam placed by engineers.

"What's the next move, boss?" Tyler asked.

Bird looked around with his flashlight. "I don't know. I'm looking for a sign. Something that would let us know we are on the right track."

Moments of silence followed.

The air was cold, but the silence felt colder.

Tyler watched as Robyn waved her light around, looking for a clue. "What's that?" she said, stopping her flashlight at the furthest wall, behind the support beam of a rock.

Tyler stepped forward and focused on what she was pointing at. "I don't see anything."

Robyn dropped her hand and moved forward. Instantly, Tyler felt abandoned. He raced behind her to catch up.

As the group of three approached the wall, Tyler saw it. Something was written on the wall. It blended into the wall from their vantage point back at the pool. Luckily, Robyn saw it. However, the closer they approached, the more apparent it became. Large letters, maybe a hand's length tall, were carved into the stone.

Bird was the first at the wall. He brushed a finger against the wall, feeling the grooves of the letters.

Tyler slowly glided his light across the rock wall. Trying to make out the words in his head.

"What do you think it means?" Robyn asked.

Tyler exchanged a glance with Bird, which was met with a shrug.

The three of them stepped back and—with all of their beams focusing on different parts of the wall—were able to make out the top two lines.

With a shaky voice, Robyn began to read aloud, "Blood for blood, a life for a life."

The group readjusted their lights to read the bottom two lines.

Robyn continued, "In exchange for what's been done, please return a lov–"

"Don't finish that," a voice demanded from the darkness.

Tyler felt his stomach drop into his ass. His heart sprang to life, as if it had been momentarily put to rest with the words carved into the wall.

Like a reflex, all three beams flashed towards the voice.

Behind a pile of rocks, out stepped a pale, tall woman. Her hair was brown and long. Her face was covered in scratches and bruises. Her lips were bloodied and cracked. "Trust me," she said.

"Who the fuck are you?" Bird asked. Tyler's gaze never lifted from the woman, but he felt Bird slip behind him.

The woman covered her face from the lights that were drowning her. "Do you mind?"

Bird looked back at him, then to Robyn. "Just Tyler."

Robyn and Bird both dropped their beam to the woman's feet. It was an almost synchronized move. It looked like something they had practiced together for hours. Tyler kept his weaker light fixed on her.

"Who are you?" Tyler asked.

The woman stepped forward. "My name is Kami."

Bird almost moved closer. "We are looking for another group down here. Corey and Hali would be with a couple friends." He raised his hand a couple inches above his head. "Corey is tall with a shitty goatee. The girl is way out of his league."

Kami smiled and said, "Yes, I've seen them."

Tyler shot a look over to Bird, who returned the glance.

"Do you know where they are? Are they okay?" Bird asked. His voice came out rushed and without breath.

Kami stepped all the way into the group. "Do you have anything to drink? I am so thirsty."

Bird unzipped his pack and tossed her his water bottle.

Kami caught it and began to drink. She guzzled it like she'd been stranded in the desert for weeks.

Finally, she lowered the water bottle and handed it back to Bird as she wiped moisture from her lips. "He's fine. They sent me for help."

"Why? What happened?" Robyn chimed in.

"I was part of the group that came in with them. I'll explain it on the way, but with extra help we should be able to get them out of here. Follow me," Kami said as she turned and moved back towards the dark corner she came from.

Without hesitation, the men moved forward. Tyler felt an arm grab his elbow and pull him back.

"Maybe we should go back and get help. Bird will be enough for them," she said. Even with the minimal light, Tyler could see the fear in her eyes. The same look she gave him as he passed through the small hole. "Something doesn't feel right," she whispered.

Kami turned back to the group. "No, we will need all three of you if we are going to get them all evacuated. They don't have enough time for us to pray that we find help."

Tyler looked at his wife, then moved his gaze to Bird, who mouthed *please* to him. Tyler returned his look to his wife.

She closed her eyes tightly and squeezed his elbow with as much strength as Tyler had ever felt from her grip. She exhaled a long push of air before saying, "Fine. Fine, we should follow them."

Tyler kissed her on the forehead, "Let's go."

He grabbed her hand and together they moved deeper into the cavern.

Three.

Kami moved at a speed that was difficult to match. She didn't turn her head to make sure the group was keeping pace. She just kept moving. Like the Energizer Bunny without the drum. Even as she snuck between a crack that entered a hallway of rock and dirt, she never turned back.

Robyn let go of her husband's hand as soon as she realized that Kami was leaving them in the dust. The flashlights bobbled as they tried to keep up with her. Each step, the group had to increase their speed until they were nearly jogging. Robyn tried to control her breathing. It felt like there wasn't a lot she could control down here, no matter how hard she tried. The air in the cave felt different. It still filled her lungs, but she felt breathless nevertheless, as if she couldn't get enough of it.

How long is this tunnel? Robyn asked herself. She moved her flashlight past Kami to see how far they had to go.

Forks in the tunnel started to appear. 90 degree angles cut into the tunnel like hallways through a hotel. Robyn kept moving, following Kami as she occasionally turned down a random hallway. Kami's actions had no hesitation. She knew where she was going. She navigated the tunnels like a mouse through a maze in search of the cheese at the end.

Robyn couldn't help but wonder how many times Kami had moved through the tunnels to become so comfortable with their twists and turns.

Beyond that, though, another question had been brewing in her mind. Like a parasite attached to her brain. She could feel it wiggling around. The only way to get rid of the parasite was to ask the question.

Robyn pushed up next to Kami.

"Why didn't... you..." she tried to talk between breaths, "want us... to... finish the... words?"

Kami slowed down.

Robyn felt relief as she could finally catch her breath.

"Listen, this is going to sound crazy, but trust me... this is important," Kami began as she waited for the entire group to get together.

Both the men arrived. They were doing a better job at masking their lack of conditioning.

Kami continued, "Things down here are… different."

"Different how?" Tyler asked.

"I can't really explain it, but trust me, weird things exist down here."

"I think we've already gotten a sense of that," Bird said.

Kami raised an eyebrow. "Really?"

"Yeah, really?" Robyn asked.

"I mean, we somehow got separated in a small, one-way tunnel, and there is no way this giant cavern could exist under Main Street," he said.

Kami nodded her head and turned back around to continue walking.

"Well, what about the carving in the wall?" Robyn said as she chased after her.

"There are plenty of carvings. Don't read them. At least don't read the entire thing. Nothing can happen if you don't complete the verse."

"I don't follow," Tyler said.

"Listen, there isn't a long enough time to explain it. Just trust me on that. I shouldn't even have told you that, but then again I wish someone would have told me." Kami took a hard right and disappeared behind the glow of the flashlights.

"That too!" Bird shouted as they followed. "How do you know your way through here so easily?"

Kami didn't answer.

She continued to move like someone under a spell. Compelled to keep going.

"How much longer? We must have been moving for the last thirty minutes," Tyler said.

Still nothing.

Kami kept moving.

Something is up with this chick. Robyn was sure of it. Either she was whacked out on some really heavy drugs, or she wasn't playing with a full deck.

Did she say she was part of Corey's group or did they just assume she was? Robyn found it hard to believe they'd be hanging out with someone like her. What was up with the cryptic warnings? Robyn was positive she was the same type of person that wore a tinfoil hat and browsed the internet looking for proof the earth was secretly being controlled by lizard people.

Finally, Kami stopped. She turned around and pointed to an arrow that was carved into the wall high above her head. "I've been following the arrows."

Tyler approached the arrows and placed a hand over the carving.

They were hard to see, unless you were looking for them. They didn't look nearly as neat as the first carving by the pool of water. These looked old.

"You didn't carve these, did you?" Tyler asked as he released his hand.

"No, but I noticed them as I was going to get help, and lucky for me they led me out. Which is lucky for us because I don't know if I would be able to get out of here if someone hadn't already marked our way for us."

Kami followed the arrow and turned. "And to answer your other questions, yes, we have probably been moving for more than thirty minutes. And yes, we are almost there."

"Thank God," Bird said as he hurried to be directly beside Kami.

He wanted to be first when they finally found Corey, Robyn could see that. She didn't blame him. Corey and Bird were as close as siblings could be. No one else believed that Corey and Hali were in danger, not even herself or Tyler. Bird did though. He knew his brother so well that if something smelled *off*, it was probably off.

Robyn was just happy they were almost at the halfway point of this bullshit experience.

Finally, the group followed the last arrow and turned into an area that opened up. Big enough that they now had to use the flashlights to investigate the entire room. It was mainly bare, except for a large pile of rocks that almost touched the ceiling. There was only a couple feet of clearance between them and the top. There were also two more entrances to the room; one was to their right, and the other to their left.

"Over there, behind the pile of rocks is where I left them. There is a small hole you have to crawl through to get to the other side, but it's only a couple feet. They should be inside there."

Robyn watched as Bird hustled away from the group and stormed over the pile of rocks like it was a speed bump in a parking lot, when in fact the rocks were piled over twelve feet high, easily.

Tyler looked at her and then back to Kami. "You coming?"

"No," Kami said. "I've seen inside there. I'll wait for you out here."

"Fair enough," Tyler said as he reached a hand out for Robyn. "Let's roll."

As Robyn climbed the pile of rocks, she couldn't help but look back at Kami. Was she smiling?

Once on the opposite side of the rocks, they found Bird waiting for them.

"What?" Tyler said.

"Look," Bird said. He pointed to the hole they were expected to climb through.

A light.

There was someone inside.

"Let's go!" Tyler said as he moved forward. Robyn watched as Bird put a hand against Tyler's chest, stopping him in his tracks.

"Now, look at this," Bird said as he raised his flashlight above the small hole.

Carved above the hole were two words: *THE LIGHT*.

Four.

The crawl wasn't nearly as tight as Bird expected. He was thankful for that, and knew that Tyler would especially be happy. Kami wasn't wrong. The tunnel was only a dozen feet or so, and before he knew it, Bird was popping out the other side into a small room.

But there was no sign of Corey or his group.

The small room, which was no larger than a walk-in closet, was entirely empty except for the source of the light they saw from outside the tunnel.

In the center of the room, carved into the stone, was a torch extending upward from the floor. A brilliant orange flame was burning from the head of the torch.

Bird waited for the other two to crawl through the hole before he moved forward.

He investigated the torch. The body of the stick had symbols and text carved into it. Tyler reached in and gave the torch a wiggle.

Solid.

The torch wasn't going anywhere.

"What is this thing?" he asked.

Bird moved his attention to the top of the torch. "It doesn't have any fuel source."

"What do you mean?" Robyn asked as she too looked over the burning stick.

"I mean, the flame isn't attached to oil, or cloth, or whatever else would or should keep it going. It's just burning on top of the stone."

"Maybe, it's feeding off some kind of natural gas? That could be why it exists in the first place. Someone found a deposit of natural gas inside this cave and structured this torch so that the room would have light?"

Bird rolled his eyes and said, "Doubtful."

"At least it's an explanation."

"I think there is only one *real* explanation," Bird said. "As Kami put it: weird things exist down here."

The room fell silent.

The flame danced off the walls and created a sense that the small room was burning. Like the three of them were standing in an oven. Bird felt sweat bead and drop from his forehead.

"Let's go get some answers," he said as he turned back to the hole.

"Wait!" Robyn said.

Bird stopped and watched Robyn approach a wall. She ran a hand across its rocky surface.

"More carvings?" Tyler said as they approached Robyn.

"Yeah," she said softly.

The wall was covered in an enormous carving of a looming figure that appeared to have been more likely scratched into the rock than carved. It was a tall human-like figure with exaggerated arms and legs. Its fingers were like long claws. Behind the figure was a bare tree that had lost all of its leaves. The human-like frame stood where the trunk should have been, with all the branches spread out around them and into the shape of skull.

Bird turned and investigated the next wall.

There were even more scratched pictures in the stone.

This wall featured trees and two mountains. In between the two mountains were several houses. Bird had to turn on his flashlight to view the rest of the tiny details throughout the images, because the torch simply wasn't bright enough. Between the houses were stick figures, dozens of them. They were all lying in what appeared to be a pool of blood, as best Bird could guess.

"Over here, too," Tyler said from beside the furthest wall.

"What is it?" Bird asked as he continued to investigate the scratches before him. He noted other details, including lanterns scattered throughout the picturesque image of the trees and mountains.

"This one is a… house?" Tyler said hesitantly. "In the basement there is, like, a door or something. There is an outline of man. He doesn't have any features. I don't really understand it."

"Fuck this," Bird finally said. "Let's get out of here." He turned to the hole again, this time stopping and spreading his flashlight along the wall above the hole.

There was another image.

A cave.

A cave with sharp, knife-like teeth. Like a carnivore's mouth after a fresh kill, blood dripped from each tooth. Inside the cave was another black figure, its eyes left uncolored. Though this was shaped more or less like a human as well, it was missing its neck. There was only a mound of body with eyes. It appeared more haunting than anything else Bird had seen in the cave. He could feel the figure watching him. Studying him.

It wanted him.

Bird lowered his flashlight and dove through the hole. He didn't wait for the others to join him, he needed to get the hell out of that room. Within seconds, he was bursting out of the opening and getting to his feet.

Moments later, Tyler and his wife crawled out from behind him.

"Didn't like that," Robyn said as she brushed dirt from her husband's chest.

"Nope," Tyler agreed. "Fuck that room."

Bird turned and made his way up and over the pile of rocks until he was on the other side.

He pushed his flashlight around the room, looking for Kami. The room was empty. There were few places for her to hide. Bird proceeded to investigate every corner.

"Where is she?" Robyn asked as she climbed down the pile of rocks.

Bird gave up and approached his friends. "I think she abandoned us."

Tyler shook his head. "No, she wouldn't do that."

"And you know her well enough to make that call?" Robyn asked as she clicked on her own light.

Tyler defended his stance. "I'm not saying that, but why would she hike us all the way in here to help recover Corey and his friends, just to abandon us?"

"I don't know, but that's exactly what she did," Robyn said.

"I don't buy it," Tyler said.

Bird moved away from the couple. He knew them well enough to know they needed a moment to themselves. To work this out. It was either that or stand there awkwardly as Robyn picked apart Tyler's naivety.

Bird checked out the hallway-like tube he believed they used to reach this point. He showed his light upon the nearest opening to his right and stopped. Behind the opening, he saw another one. Bird swung his light to the left and spotted another opening there as well. Each opening looked identical to the next.

"You guys, I hate to interrupt," Bird said, "but didn't we enter from the central tunnel?"

"Yeah," Robyn said as she and Tyler approached him with hands held, having finished their little moment

"What is the central point of four?" he asked.

Robyn moved her light to her left, then her right. "That doesn't make any sense. There were only three openings before."

"So, the room somehow grew an extra entrance?" Bird asked.

"Maybe we just didn't see one of them before. I don't know," Robyn suggested.

"You guys," Tyler said as he pointed his finger to the top of the entrance, "we just have to follow the arrow. Easy AF."

Robyn smacked her open hand against her forehead. "Duh."

Robyn and Tyler moved in unison, following the arrow into the corresponding entrance. Bird watched them leave. Something felt *off*.

He moved to the nearest opening, which happened to be to his right, and pointed his flashlight to the upper corner of the wall.

An arrow. Identical to the other.

As if it was copy and pasted.

Bird didn't even hear Robyn and Tyler approach him from behind. Not until Robyn cursed under her breath.

"Should we check the other two?" Tyler asked.

"No. I'd wager a bet that they are more of the same," Bird said.

A chill ran down Bird's spine. From the base of his skull, down to his hips. The hair on his neck and back sprung to life, as sharp as miniature daggers.

They all felt it. Bird watched as everyone reacted like a wave in the stands of a baseball game.

"What was tha–" Tyler's words stopped dead in their tracks.

Bird saw it, too.

At the first entrance, the first to their fourth, something moved. From the edge of Tyler's flashlight, a figure exited the rocks. A silhouette came into focus seconds later.

Tyler didn't move his flashlight. It stayed focused, right at the edge of exposing the figure. Bird was thankful. He was afraid of the shadow that made itself known, but he was more afraid that shining his light on it would prove its existence. It was like when he was a child with shadows in his bedroom; his biggest fear was flipping on the light to discover a shadow wasn't just a coat hung awkwardly over his desk chair, but an actual monster about to spring upon him.

The same feeling rushed over Bird now. All of a sudden, he was as small as he was at seven.

"Everyone seeing this?" Robyn asked.

Bird hadn't even noticed Robyn was also taking part in this experience. He'd been too afraid to take his eyes off the shadow.

"So, that rules out door number 1... right?" Tyler said.

As the final syllable left Tyler's mouth, the figure moved. It must have been sitting or squatting, because it suddenly grew taller. Now that it was towering over them in the tunnel, the top of its squashed head was just shy of scraping against the ceiling.

"Oh...my...God," Robyn said. The words felt like they were stretched out for dramatic effect, but Bird knew it was out of genuine fear. "It's the thing carved from inside the room. The one inside the cave with bloody teeth."

"What does that mean?" Bird asked.

"We are in the fucking cave," Tyler answered.

The figure took a step forward. Long steps that appeared to cover several feet with every stride. Tyler flipped down the switch of his flashlight, burying the hallway in a blanket of black.

He felt like a kid hiding from the boogie man under the blankets of his bed. *If I can't see it, it can't see me.* That is just a fact of the world. Embedded in everyone at a young age.

Bird felt a calming flood over him.

He couldn't see it, so it couldn't see him.

They were safe.

The moment came to an abrupt end just as the feeling of security set in.

From the dark hallway in the cave, two lights switched on, eyes glowing brightly white. Perfect circles that cut through the darkness like a warm knife in butter.

"I think this exit is as good as any!" Tyler said as he grabbed Robyn's hand and ran behind Bird.

Bird watched as the figure took another step forward. It reached out with a long, thin hand and gripped both sides of the wall at the corner of the entrance to the room. The lights of its eyes showed Bird the texture and detail of its arms and hands. They looked burned. The flesh was dark gray and black. Flakes of dark skin flew off as it moved, like ash from a fire. Blood and puss popped and spat out of open wounds running up and down the figure's arm.

The figure pulled itself into the room with one swift motion. It was the first time the figure had shown any degree of speed. Bird was surprised to see that it was even taller once it was in the room. Its long legs lifted the figure high above the opening it'd just exited.

It then tilted its head and looked around the room.

Bird waited to see what it would do next as it investigated the large, empty room.

Like the crack of a whip, the eyes darted toward Bird, settling on him. He was now in its spotlight. He was *found*.

Bird turned and almost fell on the loose rocks beneath his feet. He grabbed for leverage on a nearby rock and ran like a sprinter in the summer Olympics.

The spotlight followed him until he was engulfed in the darkness of the tunnels behind him.

Then the whispers began.

Anxiety.

Anxiety and fear ramped up to eleven as Robyn sprinted through the tunnel with her husband's hand in hers.

She moved without knowledge of where they were going. It didn't make much of a difference; it wasn't like they knew anything about the caves they were lost in. All Robyn knew for sure was that there was a dark figure with piercing bright eyes, and it was someplace behind her. Robyn would run until her feet were bloody if it kept whatever that was behind her.

That is, she would have kept running if Tyler hadn't stopped her.

"What?!" Robyn asked. She felt the tingle in her voice that was unmistakably fear. It was the same fear she had felt creeping up on her when she was younger and her father crashed his car while she was in the back seat. It manipulated her voice and made it quiver and bounce.

"We have to wait for Bird," he said.

Of course, Robyn answered to herself. She felt the shame climb to the surface, surpassing the anxiety for only a moment. She was so blinded by the fear of what happened she lost track of Bird.

As if on cue, Bird's flashlight appeared around the corner. Soon, Bird followed.

He flung a hand in the air, an international symbol for *go go go!*

Robyn felt her husband's hand tighten and pull as he yanked her to run again. She felt the shame subside. Only to be replaced with the healthy mixture of anxiety and fear once again.   The group ran past the perfectly cut corners of the rock hallways.

Should we have turned? Robyn asked herself. She didn't know why, but the urge to turn came storming in the pit of her stomach. She yanked her husband's hand and led him down the first left turn she saw. Tyler didn't argue; he simply followed, much as she did when they started running again.

They were a team. They had been a team for over a decade. Every move was already calculated and understood by the other. Robyn wouldn't have doubted it if Tyler had the same urge in his stomach to turn, too.

She moved without much thought. All she cared about was that she wasn't heading backwards. The tunnel felt like a giant maze. Every long straightaway was full of turns that were nearly perfect ninety-degree angles. There was no way to know for sure where they were going. Deep down inside, Robyn began to panic that they might never find their way out of it.

The large room they had originally crawled into seemed a million miles away.

"Wait!" Tyler yelled as he yanked her arms backwards.

"What?" Robyn stopped and took the opportunity to catch her breath.

Bird finally arrived, he too leaned over to gather his breathing. "What are we looking at?"

Tyler pointed to an area high on the wall in the corner that appeared *chipped*. A piece of the smooth rock wall was knocked loose, revealing a white surface that looked freshly removed. Three lines.

"Is that an arrow?" Bird asked as he stepped on his tip-toes to run his fingers against it.

"I think so," Tyler said. "But it's not like the arrows from earlier... these look like they were scratched faster, sloppier."

"Have you seen any arrows like this yet?" Bird asked.

"This is the first," Tyler said. "It might be a way out?"

"Possible," Bird said. "It looks a little new. Maybe it's a trap?"

"Or..." Robyn began. She felt the eyes of both men snap to her, hoping she really had an answer.

"Or?" Tyler asked.

Bird locked eyes with Robyn. He knew what she was getting at. He turned and followed the sloppy arrow.

"Or it's Corey," Tyler said, finally catching on. "Corey and Hali are marking their path."

Robyn followed Bird as he raced down the tunnel. He seemed like a man on a mission, because he was. She felt her heart drop for him. He was desperate. With everything that had happened so far, Corey and Hali had slipped from their mind. They only thought about the fear that swallowed them and how they could escape it. They'd forgotten the main reason they were there in the first place. It was a rescue mission.

Robyn felt her heart stop when she realized two things as she watched Bird desperately search the next four-way intersection for another arrow. One, even if Corey had left the arrows the most likely outcome was he was dead somewhere in the endless tunnels. And two, soon they would join him.

"Hey," Tyler said, pulling her arm back.

Robyn stopped and looked at him for a moment before looking back at Bird, careful not to lose him.

"We can't get lost down here looking for them," Tyler said.

"We can't just leave them," Robyn said.

"I know, and I'm not saying to, I'm just saying that if we find the exit before we find them, we have to go," Tyler affirmed. "You get that, right?"

Robyn watched Bird rub his hand against his face as he checked the opposite wall and corners. He pointed at a mark high along the wall and said, "Got it!" before turning down the tunnel and disappearing.

"You get that, right?" Tyler repeated.

Robyn looked up to her husband. "Yeah, I get that."

She released her arm from his grip and followed Bird.

The turn was no different than any other tunnel they had turned down. Like they were designed by some deranged digital artist who just CTRL+C'd his way through the background. It was almost worth stopping and looking into. The walls were clearly handmade. One or more people had spent an enormous amount of time digging these perfectly straight tunnels.

Robyn sprinted to catch up to Bird.

He didn't say much as he pushed towards the next corner, which was within eyesight. He had an objective and was going to push through to the end.

At the next four-way intersection, Bird once again inspected the corners, looking for a sloppily placed arrow.

"Bird, you know the likelihood of getting out of this seems slim, right?" she said as she softly placed a hand on his shoulder.

He didn't respond and let her hand slide off his shoulder. He pointed to another arrow and turned right down another tunnel.

Then he suddenly stopped.

The tunnel was the first to be pitch black, as if it had swallowed any light daring to impose.

Bird pointed his flashlight down the tunnel and watched as the light came to an abrupt stop.

"Why would he turn down here?" Robyn asked. "I think we were wrong about the arrows."

Bird waited to respond. He pointed the flashlight around, waiting for it to magically cut through the darkness and illuminate the emptiness in front of him.

Tyler caught up and, without any words exchanged, understood the situation.

"Bird, I think it's time to call this a dud and leave *these arrows* alone," he said.

Bird looked back at them. "I think I have to keep going."

"What?" Robyn said. "That isn't an option. The light literally comes to a screeching halt. This isn't supposed to happen."

"I know," Bird said. "Trust me, I know how this sounds, but this is the right way. I know it. The tunnels are trying to turn us away. We all know this tunnel is totally fucked. This is *it* trying to stop us from finding them."

"What's *it*?" Tyler asked.

"I don't know," Bird admitted. "Whatever is down here, I guess." He turned and walked into the dark tunnel, his flashlight disappearing with him.

"We aren't going down there," Tyler said with a finger pointed towards the tunnel. "We can't."

Robyn looked to her husband. "We aren't leaving him, either."

"This is *literally* the plot to every scary movie in existence. You do understand that, right?" Tyler said.

"Yes," she said. "And splitting up is generally considered the wrong move, isn't it?"

"Robyn, every bone in my body is screaming that this is a bad idea. Why aren't yours?"

"They are," she said. "I'm just not letting them overpower me. Our friend is in need of our help." She turned and walked towards the light-swallowing tunnel.

She entered the darkness and prayed Tyler was there right behind her.

Robyn felt a hand reach out for hers.

Her heart eased as his grip tightened.

She squeezed his hand back, and together they moved blindly down the tunnel.

Five.

Tyler watched Robyn disappear into the darkness.

He took a step forward, but hesitated. He wasn't afraid of the dark, but this wasn't the same thing. This was different. Something sinister was afoot, and there was no disputing that.

Tyler couldn't see Robyn anymore. Her small figure had disappeared with the flashlight behind a wall of shadows.

"Robyn! Please!" he hollered.

Tyler took a step forward, turning the corner only slightly.

"Robyn, this feels wrong," he said, his voice shaky. He closed his eyes and tried to will his body forward, but opened them to no progress. He was still standing on the cusp of darkness, uncommitted to moving forward.

"Ro–"

Something behind Tyler stopped him.

He slowly turned his head.

Something made a sound down the tunnel they had just left.

Tyler hugged his body against the wall and partially slid himself into the darkness, not yet ready to completely disappear within its grasp.

There was a light on the ground, small at first, but it steadily grew as something moved closer and closer.

Tyler held his breath. He didn't realize he was doing it, but he'd stopped his breathing.

He could hear it now. Something was walking down the tunnel.

Whatever it was sounded big.

The sound grew as the light spread, threatening to expose Tyler. He slipped another foot deeper into the darkness and waited.

Tyler reached down and blindly felt for a rock, finding one beside his foot roughly the size of his fist. He wasn't sure that it would do him any good, but he was going to go out fighting if he had to.

He focused on the lights slowly streaming down the tunnel. The kicking of rocks and thumping of steps grew louder with each passing second. He gripped the rock and held it above his head, ready to swing down at any moment.

Across from him, on the opposite side of the intersection, there was a spark. It only lasted a moment, but that was all it took to get his attention.

Tyler wasn't positive about what he saw at first.

There was another spark in the same spot.

Then another.

This time the spark turned into a small flame, and Tyler realized he was looking at a small white lighter. It moved slowly upwards towards the face of a man.

The man's face was filthy. Dirt caked his skin as if he'd lived in the caves for his entire life. There were dark rings around his eyes from a lack of sleep. A thick, bushy beard wrapped itself around his jaw. The lighter moved up and stopped, a finger slipped close to his lips and his mouth pursed to silently say, "Shh."

Then the flame died.

Tyler froze.

Every instinct told him to flee. There was someone else in the caves with him that he didn't know. He needed to get out of there. However, his only choices were to step into the light of whatever was marching down the tunnels towards him or into the swallowing darkness behind him.

Neither option seemed reasonable.

Tyler hugged his body tightly to the wall as the light revealed itself to him.

A gold lantern appeared around the corner, held at chest height.

The person holding the lantern took a small step forward, slowly moving down the tunnel without turning towards Tyler. The person holding the lantern wore a white cloak with a hood covering their head. As they continued to walk away, two more cloaked people appeared to follow, then another two. In perfect formation, with equal distance between each pairing, more and more figures emerged.

Tyler lost count after twenty-one.

He stood as still as possible and watched the parade of people continue down the tunnel. Tyler felt his heart thumping against his chest, fearing that at any moment one of them would turn and look in his direction, and spot him. That would be it. Tyler was confident he could fight three or four of the hooded people at a time, seeing as they were fairly short and he was a fair athlete. With his size and a heavy rock in hand, he thought it possible he could fight his way out. However, with a horde of them as large as they were, Tyler knew he would be overwhelmed by their numbers.

Tyler silently watched the group move down the tunnel. Once he stopped counting the passing cloaks, he noticed their feet.

None of these cloaked followers were wearing shoes.

Every one of them was barefoot.

Their feet were bruised and bloodied, with deep cuts that revealed bone and muscle.

Swollen ankles and ripped toenails.

Blood covered the ground they walked.

He watched as one figure walked, Tyler paid attention to the bottom of his or hers foot as they walked. The bottom of the foot was a mess. Torn to shreds. It looked like ground beef dipped in a bucket of chum.

However, not a single figure was limping.

Not one shuffled their feet.

Not one favored one foot over the other.

They moved flawlessly down the tunnel, following the leader.

The leader and their solitary lantern.

The light slowly faded with its growing distance from Tyler. He only knew they were still marching beside him in the darkness because of the new sound of something wet pressing against the loose dirt and rocks of the ground.

The sound of dozens of bloody and mangled feet crushing against sharp rocks.

Tyler closed his eyes and concentrated on the sound, hoping that it would die out and move away from him.

However, the sound didn't die down.

Instead, it only grew louder.

The wet gushing of blood filled his ears and made the skin of his arms fill with goosebumps. The sound had become deafening. It was all he could hear. Tyler cupped his hands over his ears and tried to will the noise away, all the while unsure of his own silence. For all he knew, his position had been given away by his own movement.

Nevertheless, the squishing sound swallowed his senses. He thought he could *feel* it now, as well as hear it. He was now experiencing the bare feet stabbing into rocks as if they were his own. He could feel the coarse stones digging into his flesh and pulling back the meat. He could feel the warm blood ooze from his wounds and stream down his heel as the dirt and pebbles filled his open wounds. The stinging burn of them sent waves of shock through his system.

He wanted to fall to the ground and cry.

Tyler didn't know what to do.

He didn't have a move left in him.

Until all of it came to a stop with the spark of a lighter.

The lighter was hardly in front of his face, but the flame sparked to life, vanquishing the horrible sound of squishing meat. The feeling of his feet being ripped to shreds also dissipated with that spark. It was as if the lighter acted as a switch, and this bearded stranger had flipped it for him.

Tyler tried to catch his breath. He felt like he was about to have a panic attack. All of a sudden, it felt like there wasn't enough oxygen in the tunnel. As much air as he sucked in, he swore it wasn't enough to fill his lungs. It felt like he was going to die.

A hand suddenly pressed against his chest. "Breathe," the man whispered to him. "Just breathe."

Tyler gasped for air, but the moment slowly passed as he regained control. Soon enough, he was able to slowly breathe and lower his heart rate to normal.

Eventually, Tyler stopped and addressed the man. "Thank you."

"Don't mention it," he said.

Tyler looked back down the now empty hallway. "What the fuck was that?"

The man didn't turn. "That? I don't know. Fuck, I don't know what half the fucking things I see down here are."

"Have you seen those people before?" Tyler asked.

"A couple times," he said. "They move really slow, so it takes a while for them to catch up to you."

The men stood in silence for a moment.

"Tyler," Tyler said as he put a hand out for the stranger.

"James," the man said as they shook. "I don't want to give off the wrong impression, but who are you and how'd you get down here?"

"My wife and our friend came down here. We are looking for some people. Maybe you've seen them?"

"Who?"

"Their names are Corey and Hali."

The man's face dropped. "Corey and Hali?"

"Yeah," Tyler said, unsure why the man's expression had changed so drastically.

"I wouldn't if I were you."

"Why's that?" Tyler questioned.

"Because," James said as he turned and walked away, "I was with them for the last couple weeks."

Tyler followed the man, "Wait... what?"

"Listen, if you are wanting to find them, good luck. However, there is a reason I'm no longer with them."

"Why's that?" Tyler said.

"Because," the man began, popping his head around the corner and looking both ways before pressing forward, "they are never going to get out of here."

Tyler followed him. "Wait," he said, grabbing James by the shoulder. "Do I follow you?"

James looked at Tyler's hand on his shoulder and back at him. "Your call."

Tyler watched the man walk away. He then looked back into the darkness behind him and tried cutting through it with his flashlight, but the beam simply disappeared.. Defeated, he lowered his head and followed James.

Six.

Robyn gripped the hand she was holding as she moved through the darkness.

They'd been walking in a straight line for an indeterminate amount of time.

She occasionally tried to say something, but nothing ever came of it. Her voice seemed to vanish like the beam of her flashlight. It just disappeared without a trace. Robyn tried to listen to her footsteps as she pushed through the darkness, but there seemed to only be silence.

Panic wasn't really an option, but Robyn could feel her anxiety climb as they walked together. Is this how it was going to end? Was she just going to walk until she couldn't anymore? Were they lost? If they turned around right now... would they be able to get back to the beginning of the darkness?

She wanted to turn around. Wanted to try her luck by backpedaling, but she couldn't.

In her mind, every step forward drew them a step closer to getting out. She didn't want to turn away if she was right there, almost out. With that concern, she also had no way to communicate with the guys. They wouldn't know if she turned and went the other way from them.

She worried that Bird may have led them into someplace worse than they were before. Was that possible? Was whatever was waiting for them at the end of the darkness better than the thing that chased them away in the tunnels in the first place?

Like walking through a curtain, she was suddenly out of the darkness.

Robyn felt like crying. She was overwhelmed with emotion. She could see again. The cave and tunnels were still dark as all hell, but at least her flashlight was visible again. At least the light would bounce off the walls and die in the distance. She could hear herself breathing. The vacuum of sound and light she'd found herself trapped in had finally passed. She felt a weight drop from her chest, all the while hoping she would not have to make that trip again.

If they did, at least she now knew it would eventually end. The unknown of it all had been the most miserable part of the entire experience. But with an end in sight, she knew she could do it if she had to.

It would suck, but she could do it.

In front of her she saw Bird. He was standing further down the tunnel as it bent in an arch. This was the first time since they entered the labyrinth that a wall wasn't a perfectly straight line. They were more circular now, as if carved in a perfect archway. Bird turned back and waved his flashlight to get her attention.

"You have to see this," he said.

Robyn took a step forward, but stopped when her hand was held back in the shadows.

"Hey," Robyn said, turning "Come on."

She pulled her hand, but the grip on it tightened.

"Stop," Robyn said. "Tyler, stop it!"

Bird walked back to her. "What's going on?"

"I don't know," Robyn said. "Tyler is refusing to follow me."

"Well, let go of his hand," Bird said.

"I can't," she said. As if he'd heard them talking, the grip on her hand tightened painfully. Robyn felt the bones in her hands grind together, causing her to scream as sharp pain shot up her hand. "Let go!"

Bird grabbed Robyn by her shoulders and began to pull her away. However, even with Bird yanking her backwards, she could feel that she was beginning to get reeled back into the darkness.

"Stop! Stop! No! What are you doing?!" Robyn screamed as she tried to grab the wall with her free hand.

"Let her go, man!" Bird screamed. "Seriously, what are you doing!?" He continued to pull at her shoulders.

Robyn could feel her arm being bent now. It was starting to get pulled downward, she could feel that her bones wanted to pop and snap like twigs on a branch. With her free hand she released the wall and reached into the shadows, delivering a punch.

She felt her fist connect with a face.

Robyn took the moment of impact and pulled back as hard and as fast as she could.

A figure then stepped out of the shadows holding her hand.

A skinny, pale figure.

The hair on its head was thin and stringy.

Its rib cage was visible through translucent skin. Its eyes were black and deeply sunken. Its cheekbones were sharp and overly exaggerated.

Its teeth were small and sharp.

Its hands were thin and bony, with long nails stretching inches past its fingertips. Even in her confusion, Robyn wondered why she hadn't noticed those nails before.

The figure released an ear-piercing screech before ducking back into the shadows.

"What the actual fuck?" Bird said as he reached down and pulled Robyn away from the curtain of shadows.

"That thing was holding my hand the entire time!" Robyn screamed as she followed Bird around the bend in the tunnel. "Where is Tyler?"

Bird dropped his head.

"Where is he?!" she screamed.

Bird didn't respond. There was nothing he could say and Robyn knew that. She didn't expect him to have the answers. She was afraid.

"We need to find him," Robyn said.

"I don't think we can," Bird said.

"Why the fuck not?"

Bird pointed back to the shadows. "Because I don't know any other way to get back to him without returning the way we came."

Robyn waited for several moments for her brain to catch up. "What if *it* comes after us?"

"That thing seems pretty uninterested in leaving the shadows," he said. "I'd be willing to bet our life on it. Besides, there's this."

Robyn followed Bird past the bend and saw what originally caught his interest in the first place.

The tunnel led to a cliff's edge.

There was a giant, empty room on the opposite end of a small trail pressed against the walls overlooking the plunge.. Robyn carefully peered over the cliff as she approached. It seemed to go on forever, but even with the minimal light she could make out something below.

"What is down there?" Robyn asked.

Bird walked toward the edge and held a rock over the darkness He took a breath, then opened his hand and released the stone into the void.

Robyn waited and listened for the sound that would follow.

Splash.

Robyn's eyes widened in surprise. "Water?"

"At least we'll have something to break our fall if we go over," Bird said with a smile. "Come on."

Bird knew he was being ridiculous.

He knew that he was asking a lot of her.

To continue pressing forward blindly.

He had no idea what happened with Tyler. No idea if the arrows that led him this far had been scratched by Corey or Hali. Bird was just taking shots in the literal dark and hoping that he lucked out. He was going to give it everything he had, and come hell or high water he would find them.

Dead or alive.

"Careful," Bird said as they walked slowly around the edge of the cliff. "I can see another platform at the end of the trail."

"What's over there?" Robyn asked.

"Based on how things have unfolded so far... probably more monsters and ghouls."

Robyn chuckled awkwardly. Bird shared the feeling. It wasn't funny, but it was all he really had left in the tank.

"Did I ever tell you about the ghost your husband and I used to talk to when we were kids?" Bird asked.

"I mean... I feel like in the years we've been together that would have been brought to my attention at least once by either of you," she said.

"Yeah, we don't really talk about it," Bird said.

The sound of their careful footsteps seemed almost deafeningly loud as Bird waited for Robyn to give him a sign to continue.

"Okay, I'll bite. What about it?" she finally said.

"Cool, so, I'll set the scene," Bird started. It was a story he had told numerous times. Not for at least a decade, though. It used to be a story that Tyler and himself would tell at parties to girls or jokingly reminisce about after enough beers were coursing through their veins. "Back in middle school, Tyler and I used to have sleepovers every weekend. My house. His house. Didn't matter. We became like surrogate children in each other's households. So, one night, we were sleeping at my house. It was the middle of the summer. We should have been in bed. Instead we were ass-deep in *Mario World*. It wasn't obvious at first. I remember thinking I was just imagining it, but no… Tyler kind of looked off in the same direction I was hearing it from. There was a voice. A small voice. A boy trapped in my wall."

Bird turned and watched his step, careful not to fall off the path. He looked at Robyn, making sure the moment was hitting her the way he wanted. The same way it had every time he had told the story in the past. It was strange; he was telling a ghost story while they were actively living a ghost story. And yet, she was into it.

He continued. "Eventually, I paused the game. 'You hear that?' I asked Tyler. He kinda shook his head slowly. We walked over to my bunk bed and waited. It didn't take long until we heard the voice again. However, now that we had paused the game and were giving it our full attention, we could actually make out what it was saying."

Bird waited for a reaction, the same way he always did. He'd rehearsed this story so many times that it was like a stage play. He knew his cue. He knew when to let the drama build. Eventually, Robyn hit her mark and asked, "What did he say?"

"'Am I still here?'" Bird said. "The boy said, 'Am I still here?' That was it."

"What?" Robyn's voice carried a higher tone. She was surprised by the answer. "That's it? That's all it said?"

Bird smirked. "The first night. The next weekend, Tyler was adamant that we returned to my house instead of rotating. We waited all night. We never turned on the video game. We didn't watch any movies. Nothing. We just waited."

He stopped the story. The path had thinned and he needed to concentrate to keep from falling into the dark, watery depths below. He held out his hand and helped Robyn cross. He took a moment and decided that it would be too hard to walk and talk, so he sat down on the edge of the cliff with his feet dangling over. Robyn joined him. She needed this. She needed a distraction from her husband missing.

"Continue," she said.

"We had given up on the idea of the voice coming back, and I remember dozing off. Tyler shook me awake at 3 a.m. The voice was back. The witching hour. It asked us if we could hear it. We responded that we could, you know? The voice told us that its name was Devon. He was a nine year old kid that had died in my bedroom. We talked to him all night. It was surreal."

"How have I never heard this story?" Robyn asked.

Bird ignored her and continued. "Devon asked us if we could

trust him. I remember Tyler looking at me, eyes wide, ready to answer. Of course, we could be trusted. However, I remember placing my arm on Tyler's shoulder, signaling him to wait. You know?"

Robyn didn't say anything.

"I mean, sure, we were trustworthy. We were two preteens, each with a heart of gold. Untamperd. Practically boy scouts. However, if Devon was asking us this question, it made me feel like *he* was untrustworthy. Unfortunately, Tyler didn't get the clue and said, 'Yeah, you can trust us.'"

Bird closed his eyes and tried to remember the following order of events. "Devon needed to be free. He knew he was dead and wanted to pass over to the next level. Heaven or whatever. I was terrified. Really. I was about to piss myself. I wasn't religious, but here it was right in front of me. Proof. There was life, and then there was life *after* life. Devon needed us to help him. He was on the verge of moving on, but was coming up short."

"What did he need you to do?" Robyn asked.

"He needed us to profess our sins."

"Why?" Robyn asked.

"I don't know. I was raised Catholic, so to me it *kinda* made sense. It was like, 'sure, I don't see why you don't get extra points for helping someone confess their sins. Helping someone become better had to be worth some extra inning points somehow.' So, I started. I told Devon about the time that I stole money from my stepmom. I took, like, six bucks to play some arcade games at Electric Knights. Devon forgave me of my sin. Tyler was really on board at that point, and told Devon about the time he broke his sister's Walkman and let her think she did it. She had to save her allowance and buy a new one because of it. Devon again forgave him."

Robyn cocked her head. The same reaction Bird expected. The same reaction that most people gave whenever they told this story.

"It went on for at least an hour. I'd confess, then Tyler, back and forth. Eventually, I told him the big one. The one I wouldn't even bother telling my own priest. I mean, fuck, the priest was just a fat, old man with a white collar. This was someone that I was already sold on. He needed my help. I told him about the time that I pissed on my brother's bed."

"You what?" Robyn said.

Bird smiled. "Kinda. I didn't really piss on my brother's bed."

"Okay?"

"So, a year prior, my brother, Corey, and I were engaged in a prank war. He would set my alarm clock an hour early so I would get ready for school before anyone in the house was even awake. I'd Saran-wrap the toilet so that he'd wake up and end up pissing all over himself. It was getting carried away after a week of it. He eventually let my bird, Pete-tree, out in my bedroom. Well, Pete-tree ended up eating my homework. I was pissed. Like, I was going to have to tell my teacher that my pet ate my homework. Like it was some stupid Saturday morning cartoon BS. So, enough was enough. I was going to go big. I wasn't going to bow out. I was going to make him throw in the towel."

"What did you do?" Robyn asked. Her voice was soft. He could feel the fear in her voice.

"I went into his bedroom a bit before bedtime and poured water onto his mattress. I then took Lola, our stupid blue-heeler, and shut her in his room. I waited for an hour or so for him to go to bed. We shared a wall, so I had front row tickets to everything that happened next. I heard him go into his room. Yell at the dog to get out of his room. Climb into bed. Then he yelled once he thought the dog had peed his bed."

He paused.

Bird thought about it for a moment.

This was the point of the story that he usually lied and cut to the end. He left out the most important part of the story. The part that made it his *biggest* sin. The thing that he thought about at night and it kept him up. He replayed the moments of these events well into his adult years. Wished he would have done something different, but he didn't. And for whatever reason, he told her the truth.

"Corey went off and told Dad. He told him that Lola pissed the bed and needed new sheets. My dad was a fucking awful guy, you know this. He was already ass-faced drunk by nine o'clock. I remember him laughing at Corey. Telling him to deal with it. Like, seriously, an eight year old kid, deal with it. No parental instinct. However, Corey was mad. Livid. He refused. Told Dad that he didn't know how to do the laundry. That he didn't know how to clean the mattress.

"A reasonable father would have shown him where the linen was kept and how to clean dog piss from a mattress. Maybe, even help him make a bed on the couch or something. But that wasn't my dad.

"I heard the smack of my dad's hand against my brother's face. I heard Corey scream in pain. Then again. Then again. I remember freezing. I was shocked. It wasn't the first time that he had gotten drunk and laid hands on us. However, this time he didn't stop. The sharp sound of my brother's face being struck by my drunken father continued over and over. I closed my eyes, cupped my hands over my ears, and tried to drown it out."

Bird felt the stream of tears bead from his eyes and roll down his cheeks. They ran into his pursed lips and he could taste the salt.

"Anyways, I didn't see Corey the next morning. I met up with Tyler earlier and cried to him, told him everything. I didn't have any idea what had happened. Not until around noon when I was pulled from class and sent down to the office. There, I was placed into a room with two officers. They asked me questions about my father. Asked me about the night before. I lied. I was scared, ya know? I told them that my dad had never hit us. Never placed a hand on us. One of the officers then told me that he knew that wasn't true."

"Oh my God, Bird," Robyn said. "I had no idea."

He chuckled softly. "Nah, I wouldn't think you would. I don't tell people about this. My brother and I were removed from my father's custody. We didn't have any extended family, so we got to stay with some really fucked-up foster familes. My dad had to prove to the court that he had recovered before we could eventually return home. However, it always ate at me that I was the cause of it all. Ya know? My dad had never gotten to that point before, and if I hadn't pushed Corey, that wouldn't have happened. Not that night, at the very least."

Robyn didn't say anything. The quietness of the cave swallowed them as they dangled their feet from the cliff.

"I told Devon this. And there was no response.

"Nothing. I waited. Waited for something. I remember looking at Tyler and kind of shrugging. Maybe that was what he needed to transcend to heaven? I don't know how this shit worked. And that was the last time we heard from Devon."

"Seriously?" Robyn said. "Are you fucking kidding me? That's how it ends?"

Bird smiled. "A couple minutes later there was a knock at my door. Tyler and I shot up. Our hearts racing. We carefully moved to the door and opened it.

"Corey was standing there with a piece of paper. 'Here are my demands,' he said. I looked over the paper and it was a list of chores and busy work that I needed to do for him."

"What?" Robyn said. "I'm lost."

"Well, it turns out he was trying to hang a poster or something on his wall and slammed a hole in the wall with his hammer. He was afraid Dad would see it, so he was about to cover it with the poster when he could actually hear us through the wall, almost crystal clear. He then used that hole to talk to us and trick us into believing he was a ghost named Devon." Bird smiled. "Motherfucker got us, and I spent the rest of the next year pulling weeds, doing dishes, folding laundry, cleaning dog shit, and mowing the lawn for him."

"Oh, fuck," Robyn said.

"Yeah, still doesn't feel like enough," he said.

"I mean, come on, you were kids," Robyn said.

Bird faked a smile and looked at her. "Yeah, we were."

"Wh–" she stopped.

Bird shot his head in the direction that Robyn was looking.

At the edge of his vision, right before the darkness ate whatever view he had, there were two figures standing at the edge of the path.

They stepped forward.

"Are you real?" they asked.

Seven.

Tyler followed James only a couple steps behind.

What are you doing? he asked himself over and over. Like a song stuck on repeat. *What are you doing following this man? Down here. Away from Robyn. Getting further and further away from her!*

He felt his blood boil.

He was getting more and more angry with each step forward.

Who was this man? Why would Tyler just feel the urge to follow him without any consideration as to where they were going. And if he actually did know how to get out of the cave... why was he still here?

James looked back at Tyler.

"Wait," he said, pushing a hand against Tyler's chest to stop him. He looked Tyler up and down, investigating him. Inspecting his posture.

"You okay?" James asked.

Tyler didn't answer.

What kind of question is that? he thought. How exactly was he expected to answer that question? *Was he okay?* No. Nothing about this was okay. Nothing going on was okay.

The nerve of this strange man to ask him such a stupid question lit a fire in Tyler's brain. The anger that consumed him was the flame and the stupid question was fuel.

James squinted his eyes. Tyler could see it as his sight slowly adjusted to the darkness. He turned back around and waited.

Tyler tried to peer over the man's shoulder, but didn't see anything. James didn't use his lighter to guide his way. He didn't have a flashlight or torch. James seemed to either know where he was going or he was able to guess. Using his minimal eyesight that had been adjusted in the darkness all this time down in the cave.

"Let's go," James said and he took a step forward and turned left at a corner Tyler hadn't noticed before.

"No," Tyler finally said. "We need to stay. We need to talk."

"Can't," James said without turning back.

"We need to stop. I need to know what's happening," Tyler said.

James continued straight down the path. Tyler noticed for the first time that James had a hand placed softly on the rocky wall beside them. He was *feeling* his way through the tunnels.

Tyler reached out and grabbed the man, his anger was almost turning his vision red. He could feel the anger pouring through his pores. His breathing was getting more and more rapid. Sweat flooded down his forehead and down the back of his neck.

"We are going to stop. You are going to answer my question!" Tyler yelled into James's face. He could feel the spittle fly from his mouth. Sweat dripped from his forehead and onto his nose.

"Yeah?" James said. "Maybe you might want to reconsider that." James pointed a finger over Tyler's shoulder.

He turned.

Even with his eyes adjusted in the darkness of the cave, he had no idea what James was pointing at. He turned his flashlight down the dark tunnel and switched it on.

The beam of light revealed the cave. For the first time, Tyler noticed they weren't in the same tunnels as when he'd left Robyn. At some point, they had gone from the rocky, typical walls of a cave, to stacked bricks in the shape of an arch. His light illuminated the tunnel by forty or so feet deep.

Tyler repositioned his flashlight from the walls to shine directly down the tunnel.

Standing in the center of the path, roughly fifty feet away, was a little girl.

She looked no older than eight. Her hair was braided and hung off her left shoulder. Her dress was white and blue. Checkered. She looked clean. As if she had teleported there from Sunday school. Her eyes looked up from the ground and fell directly upon Tyler.

They were black. Like coal picked from the depths of hell and placed inside her skull.

"Who... who is she?" Tyler asked.

"I don't know," James said.

"How did you know she was there?"

"Because, you looked pissed. Angry. We noticed that when she is around someone starts to lose control of their anger. If she gets close enough, you might throw a punch or attack someone. I'd be willing to bet that you might even try to kill that someone."

Tyler averted his gaze from the little girl back towards James. "What do we do?"

James grabbed his face and turned his head back towards the girl.

She was closer now.

She had moved the moment that Tyler looked away.

"She's locked onto you. We need to move and move fast. We can easily get away from her, trust me. She won't run, so even if we walk fast we will get away pretty soon," James said.

"Will she eventually stop?" Tyler asked. The anger was still there. He could feel it. Like a bug crawling through his ear and picking at his brain. However, he could also feel a small inkling of fear spreading throughout his body, counteracting against it.

"I don't know," James said. "I think so. However, she's targeted us a couple times. Someone different every time. So, I think she will stop." James looked around Tyler and patted him on the shoulder. "Okay, let's move."

James turned and walked., "You need to turn the light off, though."

Tyler walked backwards, keeping his light tight on the girl. "Why?"

"Because these tunnels will disappear and turn back into the wrong ones if you don't. It's one of the tests."

Tyler fought the urge to keep his light shining on the girl. He took a deep breath and closed his eyes.

Click.

Eight.

"Who are you?" one of the figures asked Robyn and Bird.

Robyn looked over at Bird.

He looked back at her and then the figures. "We are lost."

The figures whispered to one another; Bird could see them looking back in their direction as they spoke.

Bird stood and said, "Listen, we could use your help. If you don't mind."

Bird could now make out the newcomers.

The first one, the one that spoke, was a bigger man. If he crawled through the same small hole that they had, Bird was positive he would have gotten stuck. The man wore a cutoff shirt with an American flag plastered on the front. It had ripped at the belly button, exposing his large, hairy belly. He had a bushy, blonde beard and shaggy, blonde hair tucked under a trucker hat that said BONES BREWERY.

The second was a small Hispanic woman. Her face was chubby and thick with dust and grime. Her dark hair was held back in a messy ponytail that resembled a rat's nest. It hadn't been cared for in a long time. Her clothes were too big for her small frame. She had on a gray sweatshirt with a big footprint plastered over the front (maybe it belonged to the man?), as well as oversized, black basketball shorts with a red stripe down the side.

She was pretty.

Bird felt nervous now that he knew that one of them was a woman.

He often felt uneasy talking to women. He didn't think they cared much for him, so he didn't care much to talk to them. However, it didn't stop the fact that he *wanted* to talk to them. He just didn't know what he should say. That little part of his brain that was programmed to flirt and spark up a healthy conversation with the opposite sex wasn't fully loaded.

Still, she was pretty.

"Please," Bird said, shifting his gaze from her to the man. "We are looking for my brother and his wife."

The man looked down at her, then back to Bird. "You Corey's brother?"

Bird straightened up, accidentally taking a step forward without looking. His foot slipped on unstable gravel along the path. Luckily, Robyn was there to grab onto him before he could slide off the edge and into the darkness..

"Yeah! That's me. You know Corey?! You've seen him?" Bird took another step forward, this time aware of his feeting.

"Nope," the man said. "Not so fast."

Bird looked back to Robyn.

"What?" she said, ignoring Bird and watching the two strangers. "We just need to ask you some questions."

"Not. So. Fast," the man repeated sternly, with as much authority as he could muster.

"Okay, sure," Bird said with his hands in the air. "Whatever you need."

The two began to whisper amongst themselves again.

It felt like the entire situation was running in slow motion.

Bird was positive that ten minutes had passed before the couple spoke to them next, though it has only been a couple minutes.

Finally, the small woman moved forward, in front of the man. "Things down here are, let's just say, *confusing*. We want to believe that you are Corey's brother, but we have our reasons to be wary."

"Trust me," Bird said. "We share the sentiment. This place is trying to eat us alive."

The woman looked back at the man before looking at Bird and asking, "When you were younger, what was the name of your bird?"

Bird felt the smile creep across his face. Not only was it obvious that the question was something easy enough for him to answer, but it showed that they had actually met before or, at the very least, talked to Corey long enough to have talked about his bird in some capacity. "Pete-tree."

The two looked back at each other, then the man stepped forward. "What was the last thing your father said to you before he killed himself?"

Bird felt the words hit him like a punch to the gut. He went from feeling he was on top of the world to feeling the same way he did the day he got the phone call from Corey. Bird had spent so much of his adult life trying to push the memory out from his brain that he didn't actually think about the events unless it was the anniversary, and even then he had managed to slip past it lately for the last couple years.

"He told you guys that?" Bird asked.

"Answer the question, please," the man said.

Bird took a second to compose his thoughts. He let out a deep sigh. "He said that I needed to take Corey to school the next day and that he'd be home after work."

"Correct," the man said. "Come on, join us."

Bird grabbed Robyn's hand and together they moved towards the large man and small woman.

"So, you are Tyler?" the man said. "My name is Doug." He placed a hand out for Bird to shake while using his opposite thumb to point to the woman. "That's my cousin, Tiff."

Bird smiled at her. "Nice to meet you guys."

Robyn placed a hand out and introduced herself.

"Have you guys seen Corey and Hali? Do you know where they are?" Bird asked.

Doug smiled. "Fuck, we are on our way back to them now. Follow me."

"Do you guys, by any chance, know where my husband is?" Robyn asked. "He is tall and bald, with a scraggly beard. Also goes by Tyler."

Doug shook his head and looked down to his cousin, who also shook her head.

"No, sorry," Tiff said. "But come with us and we will see what we can do to find him."

Doug smiled at him and placed a hand on his shoulder. "Dude, Corey is going to shit himself when we bring you guys down to him."

"Down to him?" Robyn asked.

"Yeah," Tiff said as they turned and walked away. "Down there," she kicked a rock off the ledge and into the watery pool below. "Let's go."

Bird took a step forward, almost fast enough that he was on top of them. He was almost there. Only a small trip down the pathway until he was at the bottom. He was in the same area as his brother. He wasn't dead. They weren't dead. Corey and Hali were still alive only minutes away from them. He was so excited he almost didn't feel Robyn tugging on his arm.

"Hey," she said. "One minute."

Bird stopped, pacing in place and eager to get moving. He didn't want to lose sight of the two leading them away. "What?"

Robyn waited a moment as she watched Tiff and Doug continue. "Why did you lie?"

Bird looked down with squinted eyes. "Lie about what?"

"About the last thing your father said to you. Why did you lie?" she asked.

Bird looked away towards the others, before whispering to Robyn, "Because that's what I told Corey his last words were."

Together, Tyler and James made their way through the dark tunnel.

The urge to turn around, flick on his flashlight, and find the little girl was almost overwhelming. Every now and then, he thought he could hear the girl right behind him, her footsteps growing closer and closer. He could almost feel her breathing on his neck. Whenever Tyler thought about it, the hairs on the back of his neck began to poke out like tiny needles. He shook it off. No, he had to trust James. It wasn't going to do him any good questioning him. If he was going to put his trust in this man, he had to put it fully with him. Besides, the anger that he felt before had slowly disappeared. He didn't feel like a bag of rage ready to burst.

They moved down the dark tunnel in silence.

Tyler thought about repeating himself. Asking the question again, but knew that would be pointless. It wasn't like James didn't hear him. There wasn't anything else making noise down here that would compete with him. No, James heard him; he was just choosing not to answer.

Instead of anxiously waiting for an answer, Tyler allowed his mind to wander back in time to his last Christmas with Robyn.

They didn't put up Christmas trees; it wasn't their jam. The house was barely decorated inside. If you didn't know what month it was, you might not even guess it was a holiday inside. Seemed like a waste. They didn't have children, so the magic was overrated. They didn't need to have a tree, stockings, pictures of a fat man in a red suit for them to enjoy the holiday. The exterior of the house, though–that was a different story. Tyler knew that Robyn appreciated the extra effort. He would go out of his way to decorate when Robyn was going to be late at work. He'd call in sick to work and spend the entire day outside hanging lights. When Robyn pulled into the driveway he'd plug the lights in and *BOOM*, the house lit up like it was the fourth of July. After a couple years, it almost became a tradition. An expectation. Tyler didn't mind. Robyn seemed just as excited every time.

They gave each other a $100 limit on presents and opened them after breakfast.

This past year, Robyn seemed really excited for his present. She had been bragging about it for a while, saying she "killed the present game this year." Tyler thought it was cute, and it made him laugh whenever she made the claim. He was fairly confident in his gift, too.

After breakfast, he handed her a medium-sized box. He had special ordered wrapping paper (which he didn't think counted against his budget, so he didn't let it) that had pictures of her face scattered across the entire box. She got a good laugh out of that. She carefully peeled back the paper, making sure to not tear one of the many *mini-Robyns*. Her eyes beamed with delight as she pulled out the many gifts one by one. There was a custom water bottle themed after her favorite horror movie, *Friday the 13th*. A hoodie designed to look like the carpet from *The Shining*. And finally, a picture printed on a nice canvas.

It was of them on their first date. He had taken a selfie of them as they waited for their food to arrive. They were young and stupid. She'd always loved that picture. In fact, she loved the picture so much that it eventually became the focal point of their house whenever you walked inside. It was the first thing you saw when you entered.

She handed him his own gift.

A small, long box wrapped in red—

"We're here," James said, snapping Tyler back from his memory.

"Can I turn on my flashlight?" Tyler asked the question that had been plaguing his thoughts for what felt like miles.

James answered by turning on his own. Tyler nodded and flicked on his own flashlight.

In front of him, the cave had expanded into a larger space. The brickwork had become more fantastical. Bricks placed in specific patterns. Shapes and images with different colored rocks and even jewels of some kind. James walked over and lit a set of torches in the front of the room as he switched off his flashlight.

"Conserve your batteries," he said on his way over to light another set of torches in the front of the room.

Tyler did so. He continued his investigation of the new space.

He didn't realize it until then, but they had walked through a small doorway. It had writing carved into the brick frame. Upon seeing this, he rubbed his fingers against the words. They were filled with dirt and grime. The markings were old.

"Where are we?" he asked.

"I don't know, really," James said. He walked over to a bag that was tucked beside a large, flat rock resembling a bed and opened it. He took out a granola bar and tossed it over to Tyler.

Tyler hadn't worried about food the entire time they were down in the caves. He completely forgot how hungry he was. The wrapping to the bar was difficult to remove as his fingers quivered with excitement. He was almost desperate enough to just bite through the wrapping and eat the bar, wrapper and all.

"I found this place, out of sheer luck," James said as he opened up his own bar and took a bite. "I was separated from the group a couple weeks ago. I got chased and turned around. Dropped my flashlight along the way and ended up walking in the dark for what felt like hours. I could *feel* something on my tail. Right behind me the entire time. I don't actually know if whatever was following me was actually chasing me or... *guiding* me here."

Tyler investigated some of the art scattered across the small room.

"This place looks old," he said. "Look at some of these." His fingers rubbed against a colorful image of a tree. The tree was large and thick, reaching high into the ceiling of the room. The roots, however, curved and spiraled into a skull at the bottom.

"Yeah," James said. "I think whoever was here before tried to leave warnings for anyone who would stumble across it. If you look, there are several images across the room that I've seen elsewhere in these caves. Whoever put them here must have experienced the same things, or at least similar things, as we have today. However, it's all been depicted through images. Which means most of it has to be interrupted. The only actual written word is around the doorframe, and I have no idea what it says."

Tyler looked back at the door.

"It's what, then... a prayer?"

James walked up beside him and said, "I think it is more of an enchantment. To keep whatever is out there... *out there*."

"So, are we safe here?"

"As far as I can tell. I've never had a problem."

Tyler continued to take it all in. There were lanterns in a pile beside the bedrock. A stack of neatly folded blankets. There was trash and wrappers in a little plastic bag in the corner of the room.

"How did you get your supplies? You said you lost your flashlight, so how did you replace it? What about the food? Lanterns? Blankets? How are you finding these things?" Tyler asked.

James smiled and walked over to the back wall, directly where he had originally lit the set of lanterns. He pointed to the wall.

Tyler walked over to see for himself.

Using colored rocks, an image was placed into the wall. A picture of an open door. Inside the doorway was a pine tree.

"What is that… an exit?" Tyler asked.

"Not really an exit-exit," James said. "It's an exit from here, which is great, but it leads to another fucked place."

"A tree?" Tyler asked.

"An island. There are towering pine trees all over the island, so I guess whoever made the art thought that was the easiest way to translate it. Anyways, the island isn't *better* than the caves… it's just different."

"So, this was the way out you were referring to," Tyler said. "This is where you find your supplies?"

James nodded "Yup. The island is fucked. Arguably, I think it might be worse. However, one thing it has going for it is the fact that it isn't a giant labyrinth like this place. There is also food. I found a crashed fishing boat; that's where I got the blankets and some of the bottled water and food. There are also deer, fish, and crawdads."

"Sounds great, but what does it have that makes it 'arguably, worse'?" Tyler asked.

"It's hard to explain, but trust me, whatever you see in here is worse there."

"So…" Tyler hesitated before asking, "… you're saying what? Do you want to stay in the caves or risk it on the island?"

"I *kinda* know my way around the caves, and I have this safe-zone," James said. "So, I'll only need to go to the island for supplies."

"Then you aren't trying to get out?" Tyler asked.

"No."

"Well, what *are* you trying to do?"

James thought about that for a moment. He laid on the bedrock and pulled a blanket over his body. "I'm trying to find my wife."

Bird could feel his palms begin to sweat as they moved closer and closer to the bottom of the trail. He could almost make out the bottom clearly now.

The trip down was a long one. They winded around the cavern a couple times, staying tight to the edge and trying not to slip on the rocks and dirt.

They had mostly remained quiet since following Doug and Tiff. Doug had made it a point to let them know they needed to remain quiet. He didn't elaborate as to why… just that it was best if they didn't speak while moving towards the bottom.

In the back of his mind, he held out hope.

This was the first time he had anything even resembling hope since they arrived in the caves. Sure, he *hoped* he would find his brother and sister-in-law, but a small part of him always worried that something bad had happened. And having seen the evil lurking in these caves, Bird was afraid that whatever had happened to them must have been unimaginably horrific. He occasionally had to shake away the image of his brother broken in a dark tunnel. Body popped like branches on a tree. Blood oozing from every inch of his body.

No, he had hope.

Doug and Tiff had seen him. Talked to him. Hell, they knew stuff that only Corey would have told them. In the back of his mind, he was hoping these strangers were leading him to his brother and not deeper into the cave to be trapped below again.

They'd made that mistake once. He wasn't about to make it again.

Bird slowed down and walked in stride with Robyn. "If this goes south, I mean if the same thing happens to us as it did earlier, I have a plan," he whispered.

Robyn didn't stop looking forward. "What's that? I was actually thinking the same thing was a possibility."

"Kami lured us deep into the tunnels. However she didn't actually lead us to the end. We did that. She just pointed and said 'over there, bitches'. We just followed blindly."

Robyn nodded.

"When we get to the bottom, I'll follow them as far as is needed.

And if they point in a direction, I'll go. I want you to hang back. Make sure they don't ditch us. Kami was able to just turn around and leave because we weren't paying attention–that won't happen this time. Keep an eye on them once we get down there."

"You don't trust them?" Robyn whispered.

"I don't know," Bird said. "I just don't want to get fucked over again."

Robyn nodded in agreement.

Bird moved back in front of her and continued his descent.

The further down they moved, the colder the void became. Bone chilling breezes bounced off the stone walls and pierced Bird's skin. He reached with his hand and touched the wall. The grooves in the stone were like ripples in a wave, each one separated in a deep line, but thick and cold to the touch. The wall felt like the interior of a walk-in freezer he'd used to gather inventory when working at the grocery store in his teen years. Bird released a deep breath, knowing full well that if his vision was not obscured by the darkness, he'd see his breath linger in the air.

The only light source was from Doug and his small flashlight. The batteries were weak and the light was only a fragment of a beam.

Doug insisted they minimize their exposure to the outside, and asked them to turn their lights off.

Robyn even offered him her own light, one that wasn't on the verge of death. Doug thanked her, but said that the dying light was actually working in their benefit. It made them even harder to be seen.

Doug and Tiff stopped to face Bird and Robyn. "We are here."

Bird tried looking around but he couldn't see much. It was still dark enough that he could only see what was being shown to him by Doug's flashlight. He could hear the dripping of nearby water splashing from rocks into a larger body of water someplace beside them. Bird felt that familiar and uneasy chill climb down from his brain and into his chest. Something felt wrong.

"Where are they?" Bird asked.

"Around *that* corner," Doug said as he pointed his flashlight away from them and towards a dark, small hole that was only a couple feet tall. A light shined inside the hole. It moved from left to right, disappearing and once again making the hole dark and empty looking.

"Nope," Robyn said as she grabbed Bird by his wrist.

Bird softly removed her grip. "It's okay."

"Bird, please," Robyn whispered. "Why don't they go first and we follow?"

Doug looked at the hole and back towards them. "Oh, I see." He chuckled.

So did Tiff. She looked up to Doug and said, "Seems they also met that bitch."

"So, you can imagine our hesitation," Bird said.

"Yeah, I guess," Doug said. "Kami." He chuckled again. "Kami got all of us, didn't she?"

Doug turned and patted Tiff on the shoulder. She laughed and walked towards the hole, bending over and scurrying inside.

Bird held his breath, not on purpose, but unintentionally. He felt his heartbeat quicken and slam against his rib cage. His fingers started to numb as blood raced through his veins and into his heart.

A light shined inside the small hole.

A figure moved from inside the hole, but it wasn't right. Corey was over six-foot-three, but this figure was small. Small like Tiff.

"They aren't in there," she said.

"I fucking knew it!" Robyn screamed as she pulled Bird by his arm backwards. "We've got to go."

"Wait!" Tiff screamed as Bird turned with Robyn.

"We've got to get the fuck out of here," Robyn said to Bird. "I don't like this."

The two moved up towards the beginning of the path that would push them up the cavern.

Then stopped dead in their tracks.

Standing in front of them were four figures. The figure in the middle took a step forward. It was a tall, lean figure.

Robyn pointed her flashlight towards them.

"Corey?" Bird whispered.

Nine.

Robyn smiled as the two brothers were reunited.

Bird had done what she had thought was impossible. He had pushed through whatever obstacle that surfaced underground inside this cave. She was happy watching the two of them hug and cry. It almost didn't seem real, but yet, it had to be.

Robyn was aware that it didn't *have* to be real, though. If she had learned anything down here, it was that anything was possible and this could all be inside their head.

However, it seemed real. It *had* to be real.

In the moments after the small group emerged from the shadows, there was a lot of "how is this possible?" and "how'd you get down here?" Every time a question was asked, a new one would populate from elsewhere within the group.

Eventually, Corey ushered Bird and Robyn towards the small hole. This time they followed without hesitation. She felt butterflies inside her stomach. Something had gone right for a change. If this could go right, maybe anything could. Maybe they could find Tyler. Maybe even find a way out of there.

Robyn crawled inside the hole and found a small room with straight walls that ended in a perfect ninety degree angle. For a moment, and only a slight moment, she felt like she was back outside. In a very strange and cold room. She had the company of friends and laughter exploding all around her.

As she sat down on a boulder, Bird sat beside her.

"Before we get too far," Bird said as he reached inside his pocket and handed an item to his brother.

"Dude! My glasses!" Corey said with delight. "I've literally been walking around blind for over three weeks."

Robyn turned to Bird, who turned to Corey.

"What do you mean three weeks?" Bird asked.

Corey rubbed the lens clean on his filthy red shirt. A shirt that was torn and ripped on the shoulder and belly. There were dark patterns stained across his shirt that Robyn was positive was either Corey's blood or someone else's. "Yeah," he said. "That happens down here."

"You've only been missing for a couple days at most," Robyn said.

"I figured. Time doesn't exactly work the same down here, if you catch what I'm saying," Doug said.

Robyn shot him a look of surprise. She had been so fixated on Corey that she had completely forgotten there were more people in the group.

"How did you guys come to that conclusion?" she asked.

"Well, for starters, you just confirmed it," Hali said with a smirk. She was sitting beside her husband. Her dark brown hair lay straight over her shoulders. Hali had a contagious smile that could easily light up any dark room. She was always happy and the life of the party. They were genuinely happy people. "We didn't know for fact, but we were going off our boy Hector's experience."

Robyn followed Hali's gaze to the corner of the room.

"What are you looking at?" Robyn asked.

"Hector," Hali answered.

Robyn looked over to Bird who turned his head from the corner of the room back towards her. "I don't see anyone."

Hali chuckled. "You will. When he is ready."

"Yeah, so I'm just going to put that information to the side and press forward," Bird said.

"Probably for the best," Corey said. He reached below him and grabbed a water bottle from a backpack, tossing it in the air towards Bird. "Hector was here for over three years, he claimed."

"How could that be possible?" Robyn asked.

"As Doug said, time doesn't exactly work the same down here. He told us the day he went missing, and we have really no reason to not believe him. Hector had entered the cave only a year from when we entered, but for him it was over three," Corey said.

"Three years and three months," Hali said. "To be exact."

"How did you know he wasn't lying? How would he even know how many days he had been down here? You'd lose track of days... I mean, I would," Robyn said.

Corey reached into his pocket and pulled out his phone. "Like this."

He swiped the screen to life, revealing the homescreen.

The date was three weeks into the future.

"According to all of our phones, we have been down here long enough that three weeks have passed," Corey said.

Robyn tried to process the information. It didn't make sense, but she had the default of *anything can happen down here* already locked and loaded.

"What happened to Hector?" Bird asked.

"He died," Hali said. "A couple days after we met him. He was taken in the middle of the night… we never found his body."

"And he is currently *here* with us?" Bird asked.

"He showed back up a couple days later," Corey said. "Actually, he didn't know he'd died until he climbed back into the hole and we didn't interact or talk to him for a couple days. Eventually, one by one, we started to see him."

An uneasy silence settled across the room.

A breeze blew through them. It was cold, originating from the back corner of the room. The corner that Hector had apparently been standing in.

"Can I ask something?" a blonde female said from behind Corey.

Once again, the shock of another voice set Robyn on edge.

The woman smiled and chuckled softly. "We are all happy you are down here. I know that I can say that for everyone. I just want to know how you found us?"

"We followed arrows that had been placed on the top of the ceiling… we met Doug and Tiff and they guided us the rest of the way," Bird said.

Corey smiled. "We've been marking the tunnels as we explore them. To help us find our way back. Didn't think about the fact that it would guide people to us."

"That's all fine and all, but what if someone we don't want to find us does the same thing?" a man beside the blonde woman asked.

"Then, we do what we always do," Corey said. "We hide, fight, or run."

"All great options," Doug said.

Robyn took in the room.

She stood and extended her hand. "My name is Robyn."

The female shook it. "Claire." She released Robyn's hand and pointed to the man beside her. "This is my husband, James."

James smiled back through a rough, brown beard. His body was beaten and bruised, but that didn't seem uncommon. Everyone looked a little rough.

James reached out and took her hand. "Nice to meet you."

"Listen, it's getting late," Corey said. "I think we could all do with some rest. Anything else that needs to be discussed can come in the morning."

"That… sounds fucking awesome," Bird said.

"I'll take the first shift," Corey said. "Who is taking second and third?"

The group was quiet.

"Shifts?" Robyn asked.

"We found that *things* are less likely to surprise us if we have someone staying awake through the night. We do three rotations of two-and-a-half hours," Hali said.

"Sounds like a good idea," Bird said.

"So, who is taking the other shifts?" Corey asked again.

"I'll take the second shift," Doug said.

"I'll take the last one," Hali said.

Corey nodded to Robyn and Bird. "Good, then I guess we should get some z's."

"Wait," Robyn said. "We lost Tyler down here."

Corey's brows raised. "Your husband?"

She nodded.

Corey looked over to Doug and Tiff. "Didn't see him out there while you were mapping the tunnels?"

Doug and Tiff said nothing.

Corey reached out with his hand and said, "Robyn, if he is out there, we will find him."

"Yeah we will," James said. "I was missing for two days before they managed to find me."

"Barely," Claire said. "You were shaking and hardly able to move when we found you. Plus, you were naked."

"Yeah, well," James said with a smile, "only a couple of those things weren't on purpose."

The group laughed in unison. It was good, the laughter.

Robyn leaned her back against a large rock and closed her eyes. She passed out as the laughter echoed throughout the room.

James moved across the room and swung his foot out softly to nudge Tyler awake.

He waited a moment for the man to respond before trying again with a little more force.

Tyler stirred awake. He looked confused for a moment, but then James could see the pieces falling into place for Tyler. He suddenly sprung forward in a panic.

"Oh, my God," Tyler said. "I... I didn't mean to fall asleep."

James smiled and moved back to bedrock he'd used for sleeping, and pulled out his backpack to dig through. Inside, he rummaged through the remains of his supplies. There were a couple granola bars, a half eaten bag of trail mix, a bag of chips that was only powder at the bottom of the bag (he was going to save it for the most desperate of times), and his prize jewel: a can of Spam. Still, the contents of the bag were running thin. He'd run out fast now that he was feeding another adult.

"It's fine," James said. "You needed the rest. It was probably well overdue."

Tyler sat up as James walked over to hand him a granola bar. "Thanks," Tyler said. "I had just the most random dreams."

"Yeah," James said as he peeled his own bar and took a bite. "You will have those here."

"It was... I can't really describe it," Tyler said as he slowly opened the bar. "I was outside the cave. I could hear waves crashing. My skin wasn't wet, but it was moist, like when you are walking through a thick fog and your body becomes dampened."

James chuckled. "And you saw a mountain. A large, overshadowing mountain."

Tyler's eyes grew wide. "Exactly."

"And then you saw it. A statue."

"And it was calling my name," Tyler said.

James stood up and threw the backpack over his shoulder, looping an arm in each strap. He reached a hand out to help Tyler to his feet. "That's the only part that is different. It's the only dream we have down here, everyone shares it. However, at the end, the statue always whispers something different to everyone."

Tyler stood and finally took a bite of his granola bar. "What did it say to you?"

James walked over to the torches and killed the first one. He thought about it for a moment. He remembered when he first started having the dream. The group didn't talk about it for a while, but then Hali finally brought it up. The group, one by one, started sharing them in the morning, hoping there would be something within the shared vision that could get them free.

Unfortunately, James had already lost the group by the time he fully understood that the dreams were of the outside world beyond the door he had found. The door that would lead them to the island. The dreams were not to help them escape, but to lure them there. It made him sad that the rest of the group didn't know. They were still hanging on to hope that the dreams meant something helpful. If his friends were still alive, that was.

James switched on his flashlight and signaled for Tyler to do the same. Then he snuffed out the last torch. The room instantly felt cold and unwelcoming. The dark felt like a living, breathing thing in the caves. It was always there... waiting for him, even in the one place he actually felt safe.

He walked to the doorway and ran his hands across the markings along the frame, a habit he had found himself doing every time he left.

James turned back and replied, "It told me my wife was going to die... by my hands."

He looked back at Tyler. His eyes were wide. His mouth opened and shut as if he wanted to say something but had changed his mind.

"It told me I was going to kill my wife."

Ten.

Tink! Tink! Tink!

Roybn rolled awake as the sound bounced off the small walls.

The laughter she had fallen asleep to was gone. She looked around the room as her eyes adjusted to the darkness. The last thing she remembered seeing was the group sitting and sharing stories. Laughter and excited yells woke her occasionally, but they brought a smile to her face every time. It reminded her of camping with Tyler and friends. Up all night laughing and giving each other shit until the night came to an end.

Tink! Tink! Thunk!

The room was empty now.

She searched the foggy haze in front of her eyes and tried making out the scene before her. There were a couple figures laying in various locations across the room. She ran her hand along the ground beside her and felt Bird's sleeping form.

There was movement somewhere in front of her.

Tink! Tink! Tink! Thunk!

She could see something at the edge of the room. Robyn felt around the dark for her flashlight, trying not to make too much noise.

Robyn felt the cold steel of the Maglite. She picked it up and pointed it forward with some hesitation. She didn't know why, but something inside her wasn't ready to see what was there. After everything she had seen in the caves, she was afraid of what could be next.

Still, the group had survived long enough. They had managed to make it this far; she had to push back the thoughts and just let them lead.

Then it hit her.

Her eyes had spent too long adjusting. The room was dark. It wasn't supposed to be. Someone was supposed to be on shift watching over them. That's what she remembered them discussing before she fell asleep.

Her fingers trembled as she tried to find the button on the flashlight.

Tink! Tink!

The flashlight exploded with a bright beam that cut through the darkness like a hot knife through butter.

At the end of the room she saw a figure, hunched over, who she believed was Doug. The figure wore brown rags, but the skin that showed was bone thin and white. Like a shrinkwrap pulled over the skin. The arms and legs were covered in boils and sores. Blood pooled under the paper thin skin, and green puss streamed from holes around the ankles.

The figure slowly turned to face her.

Its thin face wore large, round glasses that covered most of its face. The cap of its skull was scabbed and bruised. There weren't any eyebrows or facial hair along the face. Its mouth hung low, a dry tongue having slipped out.

The figure turned towards Doug. It reached down to the ground beside its knee. There was a small, old hammer and a metal pick of some kind at its feet, surrounded by blood. The figure picked up both, one in each hand.

Robyn froze. She could feel her hands shaking, causing the light to bob around the room. She wanted to scream. Wake everyone up. She wanted to scream for Doug specifically, to wake him before it was too late.

But nothing came out. Though her mouth was wide open, nothing escaped from her lungs. She could do nothing but watch.

The figure grabbed Doug's mouth and placed the pick inside, up against a back tooth. It raised the small hammer and, with a crack of its wrist, punched the pick.

Tink! Tink! Thunk!

The figure slowly placed the tools back down on the ground.

It reached two bony fingers into Doug's mouth and wiggled them back and forth until it pulled out a molar. It slowly turned its head towards Robyn and raised the tooth to its open mouth and began to chew on it.

As if a switch was flipped, she could feel her voice come back to her. The words flooded from her mouth like a wave crashing to the earth. "Stop!"

She felt Bird stir awake beside her, and through her peripheral vision, she saw others move as they too awoke.

The figure chewed on the tooth and then slowly turned back to Doug, who was still sleeping. It picked up the tools from the ground and methodically placed them against Doug's front tooth.

Robyn looked around the room at the rest of the party.

Their mouths hung open, also trying to scream but failing to produce a sound.

She could see the fear in Bird's eyes. The same fear that she was positive he was seeing back in her own eyes.

She tried to move her feet. To get up and do something, but they felt like they were in cement. They didn't move. They didn't respond to her commands.

"Get off him!" Robyn screamed. "Get the fuck off him!"

The figure raised the small hammer and threw it forward.

Tink!

"Doug!"

Tink!

"Stop it! Stop it!" she screamed. Robyn threw the flashlight around the room and saw that everyone was trying to scream with her. Just like she had before and was unable to. They weren't moving either, so Robyn now assumed that they couldn't either.

Thunk!

Robyn swung the light back over and watched as the figure placed the tools on the ground and once again brought forward the bony fingers into Doug's mouth. It pinched the front tooth and began to wiggle it until it pulled free.

The figure brought the tooth to its mouth and, once again, began to chew it.

Robyn's legs finally came to life. She could move them once again.

All at once, the room was a theater of chaos as everyone else was now able to talk. Screams and shouts filled the room.

Robyn slowly moved to her feet.

"Stop him!" Tiff screamed behind tearful eyes.

Robyn looked around the room, only fast enough to find the nearest object that seemed like it would work in a self-defense situation: a rock. She lifted the rock over her head and charged towards the figure.

The figure, once again, picked up the pick and hammer to slowly glide them towards Doug's mouth.

Robyn swung the rock with as much force as she could manage. It smashed against the figure's skull. She could feel the bone inside the skull collapse as the rock stuck. Blood and dirt shot into the air, splattering her face and blinding her for the moment.

She wiped away the blood and then dropped the rock to the ground. She moved to shake Doug awake. Whatever had stopped the group from screaming or moving must have kept Doug silent and still also. The trauma of his teeth being splintered in his mouth must have knocked him out. Robyn couldn't imagine the pain he had gone through.

His face was bruised and damaged in an ungodly manner. Clots of blood chunked in his mouth and several missing teeth made black holes in his mouth. A purple bruise spread across the opening of his mouth from where the figure had peeled back his mouth with no remorse to his well-being.

He wasn't waking.

Robyn looked back at the figure lying on the ground.

It wasn't moving. Its face was caved in from where the rock had collided with his skull. Its face was frozen as it was the second it had been ready to smack another tooth out of Doug's mouth.

Robyn heard movement behind her. She turned around to see what was the center of the noise. In the heat of the moment, she had placed her flashlight on the ground and illuminated the figure hovering over Doug. Now, she stood exactly as it did. She was blinded by the high intensity of the flashlight. She used one free hand to shield the light from her eyes.

"Is he alive?" someone asked.

Robyn squinted as Corey approached. She turned back to Doug, placing two fingers to his throat and said, "Yeah, I think so."

"We need to get out of here," someone else said. The owner of the voice stepped into the light and Robyn was able to see it was Hali who'd spoken.

Corey reached down and grabbed Doug under his armpits. "Somebody grab his legs."

Bird moved past Robyn and grabbed Doug's leg to lift him with Corey in the direction of the small exit.

Robyn walked back towards her flashlight to retrieve it and examine the small room. She watched as people moved towards the exit until there was only Claire and James remaining.

"Come on. Let's move," she said as she followed the group out of the small hole at the front of the room.

James lingered for a moment.

Robyn approached him. "What was that?" she asked.

James shrugged. "We call him the mole-man. He has snuck up on us a couple times recently. We didn't know what he was trying to do."

"I think we have an idea now," Robyn said.

James smiled.

The smile seemed to linger. It stretched across his face and made Robyn's stomach ache. It seemed forced, like the kind of smile a toddler would fake for a preschool picture they'd rehearsed with their parents.

James waited for the crowd to move through the hole before joining them.

Robyn was the last to leave. She walked past the mole-man, stopped, and turned back to his body. She grabbed the blood-soaked rock and raised it over her head. She threw it down directly on the mole-man's face. Blood shot through the air as the stone connected with the creature's face. Robyn lifted the rock again and threw it down with as much force as she could manage.

Again.

And again.

Robyn continued to throw the rock down until blood stopped splattering into the air. Until the head of the figure was nothing but a collection of unidentifiable items chunked together in a mound of mud and dirt.

"Fucking bitch," she muttered as she dropped the rock to her feet and began towards the exit to join the group.

James walked through the entrance of the safe room where he had spent the majority of his time alone and safe.

Every time he passed its threshold, he felt a wave of anxiety creep upon him.

There was never a guarantee that he would be back. There had been numerous "close calls" since he was first separated from the group. He had spent many days sprinting through endless hallways and fighting his way back, only to make it by the skin of his teeth.

Still, he pressed forward.

He moved with his flashlight shining and guiding his way. He watched as the second beam of light reflected off the wall, investigating the surroundings.

"Where are we going?" Tyler asked.

"I want to show you something," James said. "It could help you survive longer down here if something were to happen to me."

Silence swallowed the men as they moved. The silence said it all. It was a mixture of curiosity and thankfulness. Tyler wasn't a man of many words, as James had discovered, but was very logical. He didn't follow his group into the unknown darkness of the tunnel. He hid to the best of his ability as the cloaked cult marched past him. James was positive that with a little nudge he was very capable of surviving whatever was down here... maybe not forever, but hopefully long enough to get out. To find the exit that alluded James. It existed. James knew it in his gut. He just needed to find it.

They pushed their way through a tunnel that had become all too familiar to James, and yet he knew it was going to be mesmerizing to Tyler.

After the doorway to their shelter, they turned down one of four tunnels, the third to the right. It moved at a perfect forty-five degree angle, slowly morphing from stoney brick into a carefully crafted ruby and gold brick.

The men moved in silence down the hallway.

"Remember which turn we made. Don't go down the first or fourth tunnel, you'll be lucky to make it back alive," James said. "I know I was."

"What was down there?" Tyler asked.

"Well, the first tunnel was..." He paused, trying to find the best way to describe it. "... a staircase made of flesh stitched together. A black-hooded man stood at the top of the staircase, carrying the heads of those I love. He dropped them down the stairs. I actually was stupid enough to pick them up. Mourning the loss of my mother and sister. It was able to sneak up on me and nearly sliced me up with a long blade... the kind you see those Amish folks use."

"A sling blade?" Tyler said.

"Yeah," James said. "A sling blade. I was able to duck my way from the attack and sprint out before I was sliced into little pieces."

"What about the fourth tunnel?" he asked.

James thought about it for a moment. "I think it's just best that you don't go down there."

Silence filled the red and gold tunnel.

He could feel the questions form in Tyler's brain. He wanted to ask. Wanted to understand, but there was no way for James to explain it.

"Trust me," James finally said. "Whatever is down that fourth tunnel isn't worth exploring. I was lucky to get out when I did, and I'm positive it collected more souls than anything else I've seen down here."

"Why do you say that?" Tyler asked.

The ruby and gold tunnel opened into a room similar to the size of James's safe haven. The walls were also crafted with the same ruby and gold bricks, smooth and perfectly flat. The room was entirely bare, except for in the center.

"Because of the collections of skulls in the room," James said. "I don't know what is inside or why it's collecting them, but I knew I wasn't about to wait and find out."

"What am I looking at?" Tyler asked, his voice faint and far away.

James kept walking towards the center of the room.

A door made of rock and dirt stood out among the beautifully crafted ruby and gold stones of the room. The door looked ancient; James remembered the first time he had seen it. He had been running from something… something that he didn't actually see, but it was closing in. He could feel it biting at his neck. The warm breath in the cold tunnel was unmistakable. James had reached for the door and, out of instinct, leapt through it.

"It's the island," James said. "This was the door illustrated back in my room."

Tyler walked up to it and placed a hand against the surface that James knew was ice cold. "And there is no way off the island?"

James smirked. "If there is, I haven't been brave enough to explore and find it. Things get *different* when the sun goes down. I spent only one night there and realized that it wasn't for me."

"So," Tyler said as he turned back towards him, "what's the plan?"

"The plan?"

"Both of our wives are down here," Tyler said. "I intend on finding them."

James smiled.

"Fuck yes."

Eleven.

"Wake up!"

Corey held his head in his hand, trying to center himself after the events that unfolded.

"Wake up, Doug!" Tiff screamed as she shook him by the shoulders.

"Would you knock it off?" Corey lashed out. "He's gone."

Hali jammed an elbow into his ribs, "Knock your shit off. That's not helping anyone."

Corey looked down at his tiny wife and nodded. "Sorry."

He moved to Doug's side and placed two fingers to his jugular. "Wait…" His voice rose in pitch with his surprise. "He's alive."

"Doug, come on!" Tiff screamed.

Corey stood and tried to think it out. "If we were under, I don't know, some kind of trance… Maybe he was, too. Maybe he'll wake up?"

"What kind of wake-up would that be?" James said.

Corey looked at him with a raised eyebrow. James motioned to his mouth and then pointed towards Doug.

It was true–James wasn't going to wake up in any state other than in pain. His face was bruised and torn. Blood dripped from his mouth in globs. Blood smeared across his face. He was a wreck.

"We can't stay here," Hali said. "We've got to move."

"Is that a good idea?" Robyn asked. "I know I'm new here, but you guys have managed to survive so long down here."

"Because we always had someone on guard," James said.

"Who was on guard?" Corey asked.

He looked down to his wife who shot back at him with large, hollow eyes. "I was after Doug."

"I woke Doug up once I felt myself nodding off," Corey said. "Did he not wake you up?"

Hali hesitated. He could see her posture drop. "No. I didn't wake up until minutes ago."

"So, he fell asleep on shift and was attacked," James said. "Seems like he is lucky Robyn was able to save his ass while she could."

"Fuck you!" Tiff screamed as she pushed towards James, only to be held back by Hali. "Let me go, Hales. Let me go."

"Calm down," Hali said as she wrapped her arms around her. "We don't need this right now."

Corey walked over between Tiff and James, "Fucking knock it off. We've got to get our shit together otherwise we aren't going to be in any state to help Doug or ourselves."

He looked over to his brother. "You followed the arrows here, right?"

Bird nodded.

"So, we know they don't change. I think that once we *mark* them, they are kinda locked. You know? They don't move anymore."

"Wait," Bird said as he stepped forward. "They moved?"

"Yeah," Corey said. "It was really annoying. Took us forever to make any progress."

"So, we move as fast as we can. Mark every corner. Keep the tunnels in place and then we can track them to get out," Bird said. "It'll just be like a giant puzzle."

"I'm pretty good at puzzles," Claire said from behind James.

"Exactly," Corey said, his voice once again rising in octaves, this time from excitement. He felt a flurry of heat rush through his veins. They had spent so much time with very little to show for it, now they actually might have a reasonable plan.

Was it perfect? No. It was something, though. Something to work off of and they could improvise.

"What do we do first?" Claire asked.

"First," Corey began, "you and Tiff stay back with Doug. Get him some water from the pool. Try and wake him up."

The two girls nodded.

"The rest of us will start through the tunnels. We will mark every corner, hopefully locking it in place. As a group, we could get through, I don't know, a hundred or so if we keep up a good pace? We will then find our way back by following the arrows to you guys. Hopefully, Doug is conscious by then. Then it's just a matter of finding our way out. Back to the beginning of this mess."

The group waited.

Corey wasn't their leader, per se. However, he carried a weight with his stature and powerful, commanding voice. He talked and people listened. That was it. It didn't take much more than that to lead a group of people that didn't want to step up and take command.

"Good," Corey said as he looked back at Doug. "Get him some water. We will be back before you know it."

The group stood up and moved together towards the trail that would lead them up and away from Doug and the two girls.

Someplace, in the shadows, something moved. Corey and the group didn't see it, but it was there.

Waiting for them to leave.

Waiting to be alone with those left behind.

Red eyes glowed in the shadows.

Tyler stood in the center of the strange room. His eyes moved from inch to inch, trying to take it all in. There was so much to digest, but the door was the most interesting.

Tyler felt a rush crawl through his veins. Telling him to open the door. Step outside.

To run.

The feeling grew larger and larger the more he focused on it and ignored everything else around him. The door was calling to him. It was asking him to leave. No, demanding that he left.

"Don't listen to it," James said. "I know what you're thinking."

James walked over and placed a hand on Tyler's shoulder.

"I don't know why," Tyler said. "I can't think of anything else. I honestly can't remember what we were talking about before this. It's like everything inside my brain was vacuumed out and only the door is left."

"I know," James said as he removed his hand. "I've been right where you are standing. I've felt the call. Felt the urge to sprint through and leave. It's not time yet."

Tyler broke his gaze from the door and looked at James. "Why did you bring me here?"

James looked around the room. "What do you see?"

Tyler raised an eyebrow. He looked around the room. "I don't know. Red and gold. The door. The room is basically bare."

James shook his head. "No."

"No?" Tyler shook his head in return. "How so?"

James walked over to the nearest wall and shined his light upon it. "I thought so, too, but it's not. Look."

Tyler walked over to the wall and focused on the beam.

The red ruby and golden bricks were almost perfectly crafted. Straight and smooth. Every one of them was the same size. However, once Tyler was able to focus, he saw that each brick had a slight design etched into it. Nothing deep. It wouldn't even be noticeable until you were face to face with it. He ran his fingers over the designs; the etches barely registered beneath his touch.

He raised his flashlight and focused on the bricks himself. A large elm tree with a collection of skulls beneath it. A figure crawling on all fours like an animal, a trail of *blood* flowing behind it. A ladder made of blades. Every brick had something etched into it. Every brick told a story without more than a single image.

"What are these?" Tyler asked.

"I think it's the caves way of recalling events. Like a photo album," James replied.

"So, you think these things actually happened?" Tyler said.

"I know they happened."

"How?"

James walked away and moved to the opposite wall. Tyler followed.

James pointed his light and a finger towards a brick. "That's me."

Tyler focused on it. A man falling in the center of the brick.

"That's how I got separated from the group. We were being chased and I fell into a hole, separating me from everyone else. I don't know why they didn't notice or why they didn't turn around after me. Maybe they did? The brick doesn't tell you everything, just a single event."

"What kind of events?" Tyler asked.

"I think it's whenever the cave changes something or creates something," James said. He pointed to the next brick. "Look."

There was a praying mantis.

"Okay?" Tyler said.

"The next day, when I was still trying to reconnect with the group, I was attacked by a swarm of unnecessarily large praying mantises. I was cut up pretty badly, but obviously made it out. These were things that happened to me that no one else was around to see. It's too big of a coincidence."

"I guess I can see that," Tyler said.

"You ever wonder how I knew you were here?" James asked.

"I didn't think you did. I figured you just lucked upon me," Tyler said, the inflection in his voice showing his surprise.

James pointed to another brick. There was a man crawling through a tunnel, the tunnel thinning as he moved forward.

"This wasn't me," he said. "I guess there's a chance it was the rest of the group, but part of me didn't want to believe they were dumb enough to crawl deeper into the cave. I was pretty certain that it meant a new group had entered." He then pointed to another brick, then another. "I knew for sure when I saw this."

This time, there was a silhouette of three people with a tall, overshadowing creature behind them.

"We went to that room. It was a *big room*. I knew that your group was trapped in here by that asshat, Kami, same as our own. My group would know better than to enter that room again."

Tyler moved his flashlight and followed the next brick.

A candle.

"I saw that," James said. "I knew you were somewhere in the tunnels. Somewhere on *their* route."

"The culty people?" Tyler asked.

"Yeah," James said. "So, I chased after you. I ran to the locations I know they pass through, finding you just in time. This room is like a control tower. From inside we can see everything that is happening… or maybe going to happen? I don't know. Not fully. I just know that if it's on this wall, shit is about to go down."

James looked at the last brick. Tyler followed his gaze and saw that there weren't any carvings after it. Each brick, as far as he could see, was blank. Fresh and ready to be imprinted with something sinister. He looked back at the final brick that had James's attention.

A tooth.

"What does that one mean?" Tyler asked.

"It means they are in trouble," James said as he turned away from the wall and towards the exit.

He looked back at the wall.

Reading every brick as fast as he could.

There was too much to fully comprehend. The range of violence and evil was enough to send his mind into a meltdown.

Tyler turned away from the wall.

He looked back at the door and felt the urge come rushing back to him. He closed his eyes and tried to push it away. Focusing on anything to stay away.

It was overpowering.

Tyler took a step forward. He could hear something coming from inside the door. A voice? Something soft and in the wind was escaping through the door.

"Hey," James said from behind him, snapping Tyler back to the moment. "That tooth could be one of our wives."

Tyler blinked and focused on the situation.

Fuck this, he thought as he turned away and moved towards James at the exit of the room. "I swear to God, if this cave fucked with her gorgeous smile, someone is going to die."

James chuckled. "That's the spirit. Now, let's go kill some ghosts."

Twelve.

Robyn followed the men as they hiked up and away from the pool at the bottom of the cavern. Hali was trying her best at small talk, but Robyn almost wished she wouldn't. She needed to stay alert. Ready to fight or flee. The other group had been surviving for long enough now that they almost had a rhythm together. Each of them moved their beam of light at the same time, locked and loaded in case someone had to pull the trigger.

It was almost eerie.

However, the most logical conclusion that Robyn could draw was that they had all witnessed something at those individual points, and independently each person was going to check for whatever it was they saw every time they passed it.

At the top of the ledge now, where they had first met Doug and Tiff, the three men waited for the women to approach.

"You guys ready?" Corey asked.

Robyn knew Corey. Hell, she had babysat him on numerous occasions. However, she had never seen him like this before. He held himself up with, not authority, but with duty. Corey had accidentally become the leader of this ragtag group, and he had kept everyone alive so far. Doug was holding on, and even Corey was one of the first to check on him and help him from his own mistake. Corey was born for this role. Whether he would have ever gotten there in the outside world would remain a mystery, but he was here now and it looked good on him.

"How fast are we going to run?" Hali asked. "I haven't ran since high school, and even then I had to beg my teacher to not fail me."

Corey chuckled. "Babe, we will do a nice, mild jog. You'll manage."

"I swear to God, Corey, if there isn't a Gatorade stand in there somewhere to rehydrate, I'll rage," Hali said as she stepped away from Robyn and closer to the men.

"You'd drink ghost-Gatorade?" Bird asked. "Ghost-orade? Gator-ost?"

"I'd drink the shit out of some Ghostorade right now," Hali said.

Bird chuckled and reached a hand out for Robyn. "Think you can keep up?"

Robyn shrugged. "I outran you yesterday, didn't I?"

"I was staying behind to cover both of your backs," he said.

"Sure," Robyn laughed as she started doing some mock-stretching. Reaching down and pulling a bent leg upward. Then doing a small jog-in-place-routine. "I'm going to smoke you."

James was the first to go, with Corey and Hali on his tail. Robyn and Bird sunk behind, but that was mainly to observe how the team worked. They had done this a couple times, and it made sense to watch before they jumped in.

Before she could fully comprehend where she was about to enter, it was too late. She was already sprinting through a dark pocket just as they had the day before. Robyn was fairly positive that it wasn't the same tunnel; but even so, she hoped there wasn't another surprise waiting for her at the end like last time. She felt her speed increase as her nerves began to flutter at the fear of a strange hand grabbing her like before.

After a couple minutes running straight, they popped out the other end of the darkness.

"Oh, my God," Bird said. "That was a lot shorter than yesterday."

Hali turned back. "You guys must have entered through the one further up the trail. It's ten times longer. This is the shortcut. It gets you right back into the heart of the tunnels."

"What do you think is the point of the dark patches?" Robyn asked.

The group didn't answer right away.

"We've all talked about it," James said. "I think we came to the conclusion they are some kind of... fence."

"Fence is a strange word for it," Bird said.

"We've never had anything cross it," Hali said.

"What about that *mole person* with the hammer back there?" Robyn asked.

Again, the group became silent. The air was thick with hesitation. Robyn didn't think they were trying to keep secrets, but it was also obvious that they weren't entirely wanting to talk about everything all at once.

"He's always been around," Corey said. "Kinda."

"What do you mean?" Robyn asked.

The group pressed forward with a motion of Corey's hand. They walked for a handful of paces before Corey continued the conversation.

"Some things are already down there. There are eight entrances into the pool that we've found. Some of those entrances are part of large, dark rooms. We don't know how many of those entrances have a dark patch, but we do know that at least five of them do," Corey explained.

"Since the majority of them have a dark patch, we hope or assume the others do as well," James interrupted.

"Exactly," Corey said as he looked up at an arrow at the top of the wall, leading them right.

Robyn and the group followed.

"Anyways, some of those rooms have their own dangers. Some with really fucked-up shit. We've seen the mole person before, but he stays in the shadows. Tries not to be seen. Which is why we set up the guards at night," Corey continued.

"A lot of good those did," Hali said. Robyn felt uneasy about the way she said it. The remorse for a friend was almost gutted from her voice. It seemed like it happened decades ago and they were reading it in a textbook in high school, not something that *literally* just happened.

"It kept us alive for most of the nights, didn't it?" James said.

Hali lowered her head.

"So... they are a fence," Bird said.

"Oh, yes," Corey said. "I think, *we* think, that the dark patches keep whatever is outside out of that chamber of the caves."

"Or maybe it's keeping whatever is inside *in*," Bird suggested.

Corey shrugged. "Possibly. However, most of what's inside can be warded away with a simple flashlight. We've managed to survive all this time, and with the shit we see on this side, I prefer the shit inside."

"You know, that makes sense," Robyn said.

"What does?" Hali asked as the group pointed to another arrow and turned left.

"While inside the first dark patch, we pulled something with us inside. Not on purpose, but we still did so. It pulled back into the dark and avoided the other side," Robyn said. "Like it wasn't supposed to be there."

"Or worse," James said. "It didn't want to be there."

The group fell silent and let James's words sink in.

He wasn't wrong. If whatever was on the outside was afraid to be stuck on the inside, what was waiting for them that they hadn't already seen? Robyn's brain began to sprint at the possibilities, none of which seemed likely. The cave was not predictable.

At least, she assumed.

Corey and his group had been able to mark a path. They were strategically trying to find a way out.

"So, the arrows–they kind of *lock* the walls of the maze in place, right?" she asked.

Corey turned around and made a face that seemed less confident than his response. "We think so."

"What makes you think that?" she asked.

"We've done this a couple times, and we have the beginning portion pretty well memorized. It hasn't changed since we marked it. We think that's why Kami is able to lead us to the large room so easily."

"What if it's just another trick by the cave?" Bird asked. He was always a single beat ahead of her, saying whatever was on the tip of her tongue.

Corey shrugged. "What other choice do we have?"

Tiff dipped a ceramic bowl they found weeks ago into the pool, filling it with water. She took a small sip, which turned into a larger chug, before refilling the bowl and leaving towards her cousin.

"Do you think he'll make it?" a man's voice said from the shadows.

Tiff didn't bat an eye in its direction, nor did she answer or acknowledge the question. She found it offensive. *Mean.*

She heard footsteps behind her as the man stepped out of the shadows and followed her. "Do you think Doug will wake up?"

She turned fast enough that a splash of water spilled from the bowl. "Hector, shut the fuck up! Of course, he is going to make it."

Tiff watched as Hector's shadow turned and walked in the opposite direction.

"Fuck you, Hector. He isn't going to die down here. He isn't going to become one of these aimless souls that walk around the tunnels. You don't get to have any forever-friends. He's going to pull through, dammit!"

She turned, this time careful to not drop a single bead of water.

Behind her, she heard a faint reply.

"I hope so."

Tiff approached Claire as she wiped blood and dirt from Doug's face.

The walk from the pool to the location of their cave-home wasn't too far apart. It was easily navigable in the pitch-black, but with the flashlight it was faster to avoid certain boulders and slippery gravel patches.

"How's he doing?" Tiff asked as she got down to a knee in front of Doug.

Claire wiped away some more blood and looked back at her. "I-I don't know."

Tiff placed a hand on her friend's shoulder. "I don't expect you to. I mean, why would you?"

"I know. I just feel so lost and confused. Scared. I just wish James was here," Claire said. "You know?"

"They'll be back before you know it," Tiff said.

"I hope so, we could really use him right now."

"Nothing down here is going to get us. We just need to stay focused and keep Doug safe."

"Of course, I have no problem watching over him, but James is the one that should have stayed, not me."

Tiff wasn't expecting that. Honestly, she thought that Claire was scared and wanted her husband near to keep them safe. The reveal caught her off guard.

"Why do you say that?" Tiff asked.

Claire dipped the piece of cloth they had torn from Tiff's shirt in a separate bowl of water, wringing it out with red water, then reapplied it to his face. "Because he's a nurse. He would have been better suited for this than me."

"Wait… what?" Tiff said. The words came out of her mouth like syrup. Long and thick.

"James is a nurse, back home. He doesn't like to talk about it. It's not embarrassing, but he still thinks it is for whatever reason."

"Why wouldn't he step in and take over then?" Tiff asked. She felt something inside her build. An anger she didn't feel before. Anger that James had knowledge that would have been important, but instead decided to play the role of the big protector. Leaving the women behind to take care of the injured instead of staying behind and being helpful.

"I've been trying to answer that for myself since they left. That's not very James-like to not help. Sure, he is kinda embarrassed by it, but we once were in traffic and watched a school bus collide with a little blue Jetta. James barely had the car in park before he sprinted in and pulled the driver out. James performed CPR on the lad for fifteen minutes before the paramedics arrived. He saved the man's life," Claire said with a smile. James might not be the most proud of his profession, but she was. It was radiating from her. James was a hero in her eyes.

"That's weird, then," Tiff said. "That he would leave with the group."

"I thought so, too. I don't know, it's–" She paused abruptly.

Tiff waited for her to finish before interrupting. "Go on."

"He's just been kinda weird. *Off* I guess would be a better way to describe it, since we found him wandering around the tunnels. It's like he has had a hard time coming back to me. He couldn't even remember the name of our dog, which blew me away because that was his baby."

Tiff mulled over the new information as she tried to make sense of the situation. "Maybe he is just stressed out. I don't know him very well, ya know?"

It was true. She didn't really know them.

While Doug and Tiff were visiting their hometown, they decided to hit up some of their old stomping grounds. First stop of the night was Bone's Taphouse. They ran into Corey and Hali and together drank deep into the night. Doug was going through an ugly breakup with his boyfriend, Forrest, and it was a nice break from reality running into some old friends.

Around midnight, they were ready to jump to the next stop. When paying their tab, Corey and James got to talking. James and Claire were stopping through town on their way north towards Salem. They were doing a little West Coast road trip, and had unfortunately landed in Linkville for the night. Corey offered to show them some really interesting things in the town. They joined the group, stopped at a convenience store, bought a handful of tall-cans, and did some of the touristy stuff that wasn't talked about on the Linkville County Tourism Flier. They visited the oldest graveyard this side of the Cascade Mountains. Pioneers, early settlers of the area, and their ghosts supposably roamed the grounds. They snuck into the old Linkville Institute of Technology's building and looked at the graffiti of 666 and pentagrams littering the walls. They found used candles and bird skulls on the dusty floor. Then, their final stop, the tunnels below Main Street.

Corey thought it would be a nice way to top off the night. The tunnels were rich with history, but also people claimed they were haunted. Although Tiff had heard the stories, she never felt anything spooky about the piss-smelling walls and damp floors of the old WW2 tunnels.

Obviously, she was wrong.

That didn't change the fact that she didn't actually *know* these people. They didn't really have a lot of time for small talk. They spent most of their time trying to work together to survive.

James had saved her ass more times than her own cousin.

Claire was always there for her to cry on her shoulder when things got too much for her.

She liked them. Trusted them. But, she didn't actually know them.

"Hey," Tiff said. "Would you mind fetching us some more water really quick?" She pointed towards the bloody bowl beside Claire. "I'm no nurse, but that seems like it wouldn't be the worst idea." She smiled.

As Claire stood and walked away, Tiff couldn't help but wonder if that last comment was a little too harsh. It didn't matter; before she could process the possibility, Claire was already far enough away that it would make it too awkward to call her back.

Instead, Tiff used what was left of the wet rag to clean her cousin's face. The swelling was horrible. Doug looked like he'd been injected with 50 cc's of botox into his lips. The bruising reminded Tiff of the time Doug was jumped by some homophobic jocks in high school. Though Doug was a big enough man to hold his own, he took just as much damage as he dished out.

Still, Tiff couldn't help but fight back the tears as she wiped away the dirt that mixed with blood from his face. Doug didn't deserve this. None of them did, but Doug didn't more than anyone. He was always the first person to stand up for a stranger. Stand up for what was right. Tiff was positive that when Doug was old and hanging out in a rocking chair with a blanket on his lap talking to his grandchildren, every story would be about which side of history he was on. He would always be on the right side of whatever the cause. Doug was one of the rare humans that existed that could understand and accept every race, culture, cause, whatever it was. He was a good one.

And he could die down here before he had a chance to change the world.

"Ti–," Doug said with a cough.

It took a moment for Tiff to comprehend what was happening. She ripped the rag back to her chest in shock.

"Ti–," he repeated weakly.

"Oh, my God, Doug!" she cried. The tears she fought to keep at bay come flooding forth. Fuck it, there was no stopping them. They streamed down her face forming a river that cut through the dirt and grim that collected over the weeks underground.

"What happened?" Doug asked as he cautiously raised a hand and touched his mouth.

Tiff turned away for a moment to try and gain any form of composure. "That–that mole person old-fuck attacked you."

Doug winced in pain, his eyes still pressed closed. "That dusty old man with the weird glasses?"

Tiff nodded. It was easier than saying yes as the words couldn't form correctly as she tried to regain her composure.

"Fuck," Doug said. "I knew after Forrest I'd have to lower my standards a little... but a dusty, old man seems like a new low."

Tiff snorted.

Even at his worst, Doug was the best of them.

Nothing could break him, and that was exactly what they'd need to make it out.

"The rest of the group are trying to get us out," Tiff said through her tears. "They went full-on kamikaze. We are finding the way back."

Doug placed a finger under his gums, pulling back a chunk of meat and blood. "Okay, that's fine. I'm kinda over this little weekend trip, not to be rude."

Tiff smiled. "Me too. How's Eugene sounding?"

"Oh, God," he said quietly. "Not great, but a step above this shit."

Tiff laughed. "I love you, dude".

Tears streamed down her face.

"I love you too, dude," Doug responded.

Tiff turned her head towards the pool.

She couldn't see Claire. She didn't have a flashlight, and Tiff assumed she was using what muscle memory she had gained since they'd found the pool to find it. "Claire! Claire! He's awake!"

Tiff waited a moment and tried to adjust her eyes to the darkness beyond them. She reached over Doug and grabbed the solitary lantern to extend her hand out towards the pond with light.

"Claire!" she screamed with a newfound joy in her voice.

With the help of the lantern, she could see a little further. She couldn't see the pool exactly, but her eyes were slowly collecting the scene and creating an image.

"How's– Hali?" Doug asked through the blood pooling inside his mouth.

"What?" Tiff asked, not dropping her attention from trying to find Claire.

"Hali? How… how is she?" Doug muttered.

"She's with the rest of the group," Tiff said. "Claire!" she screamed again into the darkness. Her eyes had adjusted enough to make out the figure of a woman hunched over the pool of water at the bottom of the cavern.

The figure turned towards her.

"What?" Tiff could hear faintly.

The cavern was large, large enough that she felt she was at an amphitheater. However, it wasn't large enough that Tiff should have had a hard time hearing or vice versa.

"Claire! Doug! Is! Awake!" Tiff screamed, punching every word with authority.

She could see Claire adjust and move away from the pool. She was a dark shadow barely discernible from the outline of the water. "I can't–you. I–fill the–right back."

The words bounced off the cavern walls to Tiff in fragments. Like a radio transmission lost over the airwaves of endless space.

"Hali," Doug said. "She's okay?"

Tiff looked down at her cousin. "Yeah, Hali is fine."

She turned back to Claire and watched as the silhouette of her bent over and filled the bowl in the water.

Behind Claire, Tiff thought she'd seen movement, though she wasn't positive. A movement in the water that could have been her eyes playing tricks with her, making her think she was seeing something that wasn't really there.

"Good," Doug muttered, his voice getting weaker. "She seemed so happy the last time I saw her."

The sentence caught Tiff off guard.

"What do you mean *the last time you saw her?*" she asked.

Tiff looked down at her cousin. He didn't answer.

"Doug!" she yelled as she grabbed him by his shoulders and shook. "Doug! Wake up you sonovabitch!"

He didn't wake.

Tiff looked back towards Claire. "Hurr–"

She stopped.

Tiff could easily make out the silhouette of Claire, raising the bowl and inspecting it to make sure it was full enough. However, behind her, there was something new.

Two red eyes pierced through the darkness, reflecting the limited light of the lantern.

Claire turned and moved away from the pool. "Tiffany, I'm com–"

There was a splash of water.

Tiff watched the sudden movement of red eyes lunging towards her friend and grabbing her. Pulling her into the water.

The cavern echoed with the sound of Claire splashing and disappearing into the water.

Thirteen.

The group moved through the tunnels at slight jog, making sure to not overwork themselves. They were going to be in for a long day of mapping.

Corey had it worked out in his head, even with them moving at a reasonable pace, it was almost impossible to make it through everything unless they got extremely lucky.

It was all *guess and check*. They mark a random corner and follow it, following their guts down tunnel after tunnel until a turn. They would then mark the corner and continue moving.

The group had already been going at it for an hour when he turned back to examine the group.

They were beat.

He could tell at a glance that the weight of the situation was wearing at them. They needed him to pep them up.

Corey racked his brain for something to say. Something that would carry weight, like a relatable story or an inspirational speech. His mouth opened but nothing came out.

His heart raced with every passing moment.

They all looked at him, waiting for him to say something. Anything.

And yet, Corey couldn't find it.

"Maybe we should take a moment and rest," Bird suggested.

Corey nodded. "Awesome, let's do that."

The group spread out, each finding someplace they could rest. Corey found a rock sticking about a foot out of the ground and sat on top of it.

He watched the group as they split off into pairs.

Robyn with Bird.

James with Hali.

It was weird.

He felt alone, although he shouldn't. He had his wife and brother with him. Robyn had been part of his life for as long as he remembered, and he was extremely comfortable with her.

And yet, he felt alone. Corey felt a pressure in his chest. The stress of everything mounting on top of him.

Hali walked over to him, finding a place to sit between his legs. "Hey, babe."

Corey wrapped his arms around her.

"James has an idea," she said.

He moved his head down and placed it on her shoulder. "Okay?"

"I'm just saying, I know it's crazy. It sounds wrong. I just think you should keep an open mind. Hear what he has to say. I think it's worth a shot."

Corey removed his head and leaned back. "What is his idea?"

Hali grabbed his arm and pulled him closer, wrapping his arms tightly around her body. "I didn't say anything. Just let him tell you."

The warmth of his wife lifted his spirits, if only for the moment.

Hali wasn't the type of person to beat around the bush. She was very "matter of fact" and it was one of the many things he found endearing about her. However, she was also very trustworthy and if she told James she wouldn't tell him, Corey would be barking up the wrong tree if he thought she was about to spill the beans. Unless, it was something she felt needed to come out of her mouth first.

Corey waited. to see if Hali had anything to add. Anything to say that would help him understand what he was about to walk into.

She didn't say anything. Hali just pulled him closer and kissed the back of his hands. If he closed his eyes and concentrated, he could imagine they weren't lost in this hell. They were on vacation or camping, holding each other through the night and just enjoying the quiet around them.

The idea was interrupted before it was ever fully formed when James cautiously approached and said, "Hey, man."

Corey sat up. "Sup?"

"I've been thinking…" he started.

Corey nodded his head and waited for him to continue.

"I don't think we are going to manage to accomplish all this today at this rate. I mean, we've made more progress than we usually do, but I feel deep inside that it won't be enough."

Corey cocked his head. "What do you mean?"

"I don't think we are going to be able to map everything out at this rate," James said flatley.

Corey looked around and saw Robyn and Bird approaching.

"What's going on?" Robyn asked.

James turned and addressed her. "Robyn, hey, I'm just saying, I don't think we are doing enough. I don't think we are covering enough ground."

"So, what are you suggesting?" Bird asked.

"I think we should split up," James said.

Corey's head popped in the air. "What?"

"I think we should split up into three groups. You and Hali, Bird and Robyn, and I'll go at it alone. We each take a different corner and start marking. I know it sounds crazy, but it's the only way for us to cover the ground we are going to need to cover to get Doug the help he needs," James explained.

"Not a chance," Corey said.

"Don't do that," Hali said softly. "He is making sense, kinda."

"I'm not saying it's the best idea, just that we are kind of in a Hail Mary type of situation. We need to go for it. And as crazy as it sounds, it might be what gets us out of here as soon as possible," James said.

Corey paused.

He didn't entirely disagree with what James was saying; he just didn't believe in the solution. There was a lot at stake, and even though he wanted to do whatever he could to save Doug, it probably still wouldn't be wise to split the group up. From their limited experience in the tunnels, groups wielded the best results. Less things happened as the group moved together. Hell, he hated when the group sent out only a pair of people. It felt vulnerable and dangerous. However, deep inside his gut he knew that they weren't covering enough ground and he didn't have a better solution.

"How do you imagine this going down?" Corey asked.

James smiled. "We split up. We mark corners as usual. The tunnels are pretty symmetrical, as far as we can tell, so when we have each run the length of thirty or so corners, we turn back and meet here. We have essentially locked in ninety corners in the time we would have only locked in thirty, and we can then move forward and do it again… and again," James said.

Corey paused to allow the information to sink in. It made sense. They'd obviously be setting themselves up for more success. Logistically, Corey felt his brain crunching the numbers and the pros began to outweigh the cons.

He literally had just sent out Doug and Tiff in a group of two the night before. He himself had gone with James on numerous occasions.

A pair wasn't a deathwish–it just wasn't the security of a group of five.

James by himself seemed like it was playing with the odds, and the odds were controlled by the house. However, James seemed to accept that as his odd-man-out situation.

"Thirty corners?" Corey asked.

"Or whatever number you think is good," James said.

Corey thought about it.

Bird pushed through the group. "Excuse me, don't want to be *that guy*, but have none of you seen a horror movie?"

He looked around the group, his eyes landing on Corey.

"The groups that split up are the first to fall. Every. Fucking. Time. I don't care if it takes longer, we should do this logically and safely. The group sticks together," Bird said.

Robyn stepped forward and grabbed Bird's hand. "I'm with this guy. I have a Shudder account and literally every cheesy horror movie has the group split up at some point and it never ends well."

"This isn't a horror movie," Hali said.

"This isn't a rom-com, though," Robyn said. "I mean, I don't tend to watch those, but I imagine they don't have dusty old men chipping out teeth while Ryan Gosling and Rachel McAdams sleep."

"I don't think they'd do a rom-com together, actually," Bird said. "They hated working together on *The Notebook,* and the general audience would be confused and think it was some weird sequel. I just don't think it works."

"Seriously?" James asked.

"I'm just saying," Bird said.

Corey waved a hand in the air. "Stop."

He waited for all eyes to lock on him. He felt a rush of energy whenever they looked to him for answers. It made him feel like he had no choice but to keep everyone safe.

Everyone, including Doug. He just didn't know that Doug would agree with the strategy.

"We aren't splitting up," Corey said. "We stick together. We do as much as we can, but we pick up our pace. We move until we feel like we are going to die, then we push harder. We find the way out. Tonight."

Bird smiled.

Robyn, too.

Corey looked over at James, who shook his head softly.

"If you don't agree, you are welcome to go at it alone," Corey said. "However, the group staying together is our best bet."

James rubbed his face aggressively. Corey saw dust and dirt fly as his hands crawled through his beard. "Yeah, of course, it was just an idea."

Corey looked at the group and nodded. "Cool. So, let's get moving. Doug is counting on us."

"How do you think Doug's doing?" Bird asked the group.

No one answered.

He didn't mean anything by it. It wasn't meant to come out morbid or insensitive. He was just thinking out loud. Honestly, the words pierced through his lips before he could actually put any thought behind them.

"He was pretty fucked up," James said.

"What is that supposed to mean?" Robyn asked.

James looked back at her. "Nothing. I was just stating the fact. He might need to be carried out if he has any chance."

"Everyone, please," Corey said as he notched an arrow in the corner and moved. "We need to stay focused."

Corey paused at the turn.

Bird looked over at Robyn. She'd noticed it, too.

They rushed forward towards the corner.

The tunnel was different, for the first time as far as Bird was aware. It slanted slightly downwards. Just enough that they'd be able to notice, but not enough for it to be any kind of real danger walking down.

"Do we keep pushing? Maybe we turn another way?" Robyn asked.

Corey didn't answer. He looked over every inch of the tunnel from their vantage point. It made sense. If everything up to this point had remained basically the same, then there would be some hesitation going forward the moment something changed, even if it was just a small decline in the tunnel that was otherwise straight as an arrow.

"What do you think it means?" Hali asked.

Corey shook his head. "I have no idea."

"Should we push forward?" Bird asked. He hoped his younger brother had the answer. He was at a loss at what to do next

Corey shrugged.

"Maybe it's a good sign?" James said with a smile.

"Why do you say that?" Robyn asked.

"Well, maybe we've managed to make enough headway that the tunnel has kinda lost its hold on us or something? I don't know how these things work," James said.

Corey shook his head slowly. "Maybe."

"That would be nice," Bird said. "Maybe we dip our toe in? Check it out and, if we need to, we can backpedal."

"We should vote," Corey said.

"Corey," Hali said. "We don't need to vote. We just need you to make the call."

Bird didn't love that as a response. He would have been more interested in a vote. It didn't seem fair to put all the pressure on Corey when they could all talk through it together; however, it was probably going to eat up valuable time that was precious to Doug in his condition.

"All in favor of dipping our toes," Corey said, ignoring his wife, "raise your hand."

Bird looked over to Robyn to see if she raised her hand.

Robyn's eyes were wide. Bird could see something he had only seen in them since they entered the cave.

Fear.

He turned to see what she was looking at as a white, thin, sickly looking leg retracted from around the corner and disappeared from view.

"What the fuck was that?" Robyn whispered.

Bird removed his eyes from the corner and back towards the group.

"Guys! We need to move!" he yelled.

"What? Why?" Corey asked.

Bird took a step forward and urged the group to follow with a sweeping of his hand. "Something is waiting for us around the corner."

He looked back at Robyn, who was still eyelocked on the corner.

"What did you see?" Hali asked.

"I don't know," Bird said. "I just don't think that seeing *anything* is particularly good down here."

He looked over to Robyn and said, "Let's go." He reached a hand towards her.

Robyn looked back and saw his gesture and took a step forward.

In the snap of a finger, a long, white arm reached out and grabbed her by the shoulder. Its nails were long and pointed, thus piercing her shoulder. Blood spurted into the air as Robyn filled the tunnel with an unearthly scream.

Another arm then reached out and grabbed her at the waist, pulling her into the dark shadows around the corner.

"Robyn!" Bird screamed.

Fourteen.

Everyone saw it. Though it happened fast, it felt like slow-motion. Robyn had screamed in pain as her blood smeared the walls of the tunnel.

Corey's first reflex was to push his wife behind him. Hali didn't fight it, and disappeared without much effort.

Corey locked eyes with his brother. "Don't."

Bird looked at him, his eyes filled with desperation and rage. A look that Corey had never seen before. Bird was always the first to get the situation under control, choosing whatever non-violent ending he could. He wasn't the first person to dive into a crashed car, a house on fire, or break up a fight. At least, that's what Corey thought, but in the moment, when the cards were on the table, he saw something in his brother that he didn't even know was there.

A fighter.

"I have to," Bird said.

Corey lunged out to grab his brother, but felt something hit him like a baseball bat to the gut.

He fell to the ground, holding his stomach as he tried to catch his breath. All around him, there was shuffling and sounds that he couldn't identify as he tried to control his breathing. Dust and dirt cycloned all around him, as if a gust of wind had shot through the tunnels and disrupted the stagnant airflow for the first time in a millennium.

Corey moved to his knees and tried to gather what was happening around him.

Shadows were attacking from every direction. It was as if they had gained sentience and were pissed off at the group for having invaded their territory.

Nightmarish black claws reached out from the corner with unimaginable length, scratching at James. Another arm then grabbed at him from around his ankles as he tried to fight them off.

He looked for his wife and saw that Hali was right where he had left her. Her hands were pressed up against her mouth as she was trying to keep herself from screaming.

From further in the tunnel, something moved up the decline towards her.

Corey tried to scream for Hali, but he was still trying to recover from his attack. He reached a hand out for her, hoping she would move towards him.

A tall figure moved upon her, silently.

A shadow, with no features or identifiable features besides its silhouette. A tall shadow with a mess of branches sprouting from its head.

This was all a trap. And Corey led them straight into it.

The tree-headed shadow picked up his wife, covering her mouth with one crooked hand and, with the other hand, wrapped itself around her chest and pulled her back into the shadows. Down the decline and out of view.

Corey finally caught his breath and screamed, "Hali!"

He turned just as James was lifted from the air and slammed against the wall. The shadows dropped him to the ground and then grabbed his unconscious body by the ankles, dragging him around the corner, opposite of where Robyn disappeared.

Corey looked from the corner towards his brother. "Tyler!"

He looked back at Corey. He had seen it all unfold. The horror of watching the entire party ripped away.

"We need to get Hali!" Corey shouted as he tried to stand.

Bird looked down the tunnel and turned his head back around the corner.

"Please," Corey pleaded. "I'm fucking scared right now."

Bird walked over to help up his brother. "Corey, listen to me. I'm not going."

"No," Corey said as tears welled in his eyes. "I just got you back, please."

"Find your wife," Bird said. The confidence in his voice was strict and to the point. "I'm going to get Robyn. I can't lose her. Get Hali and meet us back at the pool."

Corey wiped the tears from his eyes and nodded in acknowledgment of the plan.

Bird wrapped his arms around him and they hugged. It was fast, but strong.

Bird nodded to his brother, then moved and disappeared beyond the corner that had swallowed Robyn moments earlier.

Corey took only a moment to gain his composure before he

pushed away and down towards Hali. Hoping he could outrun whatever it was that had his wife.

If he'd known this would be the last time he saw his brother, he would have held on for a moment longer. Held him a little stronger. But he didn't do any of it.

Instead, Corey pushed down towards the decline and into the unknown.

Fifteen.

The water was cold.

Claire didn't have time to hold her breath as her body was ripped below the water.

Her initial thought was that she had slipped, falling backwards and into the water behind her. However, as she struggled to get fully out of the water, she felt the tightening of a hand around her ankle. Every attempt to free herself only made the hand grip harder. Her skin screamed much as she did from the nails of the hand piercing her flesh.

Claire kicked her free leg down towards whatever was holding her under, connecting with the hand and temporarily releasing her. It was just enough time for her to breach the surface. She coughed and tried to suck in as much air as possible, knowing in the back of her head she was about to get yanked below again.

The water calmed as she stopped struggling.

She looked off to the shore and saw Tiff running down the path towards her. She was screaming something that Claire couldn't make out—she was too busy trying to catch her breath and push out any water that had slid down into her lungs with deep, brutal coughs.

Claire was further than she figured she should be from the rocky shoreline of the pool. In fact, she was further out than anyone in the group had ever dared to explore. She dipped her toe down and realized that she couldn't touch the rocky bottom below. Panic set in as she understood that whatever it was wasn't trying to drag her under, but drag her further away from Tiff.

Make her vulnerable.

Claire cautiously floated in a circle, looking for any movement in the water.

The only ripples in the water were those that she caused herself.

"Claire!" Tiff screamed from the shore. "Swim!"

Claire took a moment and continued to look for whatever it was that was about to attack her. She wasn't stupid, she knew it was coming. She just didn't know from where it would appear. Claire had spent enough time in the cave to know this wasn't over. She might get lucky and fight her way to the shore, but it would be just that.

A fight.

After not being able to pinpoint any danger or anything even mildly suspicious, she decided to follow Tiff's advice and swim towards the shore.

She leaned forward and began to stroke forward as her feet kicked fiercely behind her. Claire rotated her head with each reach forward of her arm. Her ankles burned as the fresh cuts filled with the stale water she cut through.

"Wait!" Tiff screamed.

Claire pulled back and waited, dipping her toe down again, still not finding the floor.

"What?" Claire screamed back.

She waited for Tiff to respond, but her response came later than it should have.

"I don't know," Tiff finally answered. "I thought I saw something."

Claire waited for a moment longer before giving up and deciding she had to just push through. She couldn't be more than fifty yards away from Tiff. She could swim that length.

She reached an arm forward, pulling her body further and further. Her legs splashed water through the air like a small engine attached to her feet. She felt like she was skipping over the water, but when she adjusted her view, she saw that she had barely moved. Tiff was still at least forty yards away.

Bubbles began to pop as they reached the surface in front of her.

"Oh, no," Claire said to herself.

There were more bubbles a few feet to her left. Then more to her right, and even more behind it.

Soon enough, Claire lost track of the number of streams of bubbles popping around her.

"Are you seeing this?" Claire screamed.

"Get the fuck out of there!" Tiff yelled.

Claire hunched forward and began to swim through the pits of bubbles, trying to avoid them when she could, but cutting straight through them when she couldn't.

A large object bobbed to the surface beside her. Claire pushed through, trying to avoid it. As she rotated her head, she saw something else pop up out of the water to her right, and when she moved her head with her stroke, she saw something pop up to her left.

From every direction, she was seeing and feeling something crash through the surface of the water.

She was surrounded.

Claire kept swimming. She couldn't be more than twenty yards away. She was almost there.

She reached her left arm forward to propel her body forward just as something popped to the surface in front of her. Her arms wrapped around the object, causing her to instinctively push backwards. Claire settled in the water as she tried to gain her composure.

The water was full of similarly shaped figures. She was outnumbered. The water was thick with white figures that surrounded her.

"Oh, my God," Claire gasped.

"What?! What is it?" Tiff screamed from the shore.

Claire could see it now.

Directly in front of her, to her left, to her right, as far as she could see, covering every inch of water as far as she knew, were bloated, blueish-white, slimy, dead bodies. The face in front of her was a child, no older than ten. His eyes wide open, but the color inside them was as dead as he was. A white film stretched over his sockets, leaving them swollen and broken. The boy's skin was wrinkly and stretched over his water-logged body. His mouth was slightly ajar, his thick tongue sticking out slightly.

Claire averted her gaze, but couldn't find any place where there wasn't a dead body floating beside her.

There was a beautiful middle-aged woman. A skinny Black man with short black hair and black rimmed glasses. A porky, older man who floated on his back, his belly rising from the water like an iceberg.

"They are all dead!" Claire screamed to Tiff. "I don't know what to do."

She tried to look over the sea of bodies towards her friend, but it was no use. If Tiff was out there, she wasn't visible over the flesh and decay in front of her.

"You're gonna have to dive under," Tiff finally answered.

"What? Are you crazy?!" Claire said.

"I'm serious," Tiff said. "The wall of people only goes out about twenty or thirty feet. You could dive under it and pop out on the other side."

Claire looked around herself, hoping to find an escape route that didn't involve her diving below a wall of dead bodies. But there was no other solution.

"Okay," she yelled back. "Here we go!"

Claire sucked in as much air as she could to prepare for her dive.

The young boy in front of her, his eyes milky white, looked straight at her... and blinked.

The image caught her off guard.

Claire splashed backwards, bumping her head against a bloated body that made an unsettling *thump* as he pushed against the rows of bodies around it.

The animal part of her brain told her to swim. To get going. Claire felt anxiety build in her chest. Her heart raced as sweat began to drip from her forehead. She had been in the water too long. Her arms and legs were becoming sore and stiff. Without thinking, she reached out to sturdy herself.

Her arm rested on the belly of the porky man.

The weight of her resting pushed down on the man's belly, letting out a *squish* as her forearm slumped into the man's stomach. The skin fell apart like it was a thick liquid. Suddenly, she could feel herself digging in deeper and deeper into the man as she began to panic. His belly felt like custard. She struggled to rip her arm free, terrified that she'd flip the man and disappear beneath him, unable to release her arm, and drown.

With a swift pull, she freed her arm and steadied herself.

Claire looked at the man. His bloated face was a round surface that completely hid his neck. His skin was paper-white; any color the man once had left his body long ago. His mouth slowly began to open. A fat tongue, like an earthworm popping through the surface of the soil, squirmed from his mouth.

That was enough for Claire.

She sucked in as much oxygen as she could, filling her lungs like a balloon, and dove below the water.

She no longer cared.

Claire wanted out of the water. She knew something was going to happen. It was too obvious.

She just didn't care anymore.

Claire held her breath and pushed as deep as she imagined she needed to go. Several feet should have been more than enough to clear the bodies floating above her.

Every now and then, she'd feel her heel or top of her arm connect with one of the corpses. She'd immediately readjust and swim a bit deeper to avoid it.

Again, her heel kicked against a body. So, she went a little deeper.

Then again.

And again.

There was no way she could go any deeper. She was bound to hit the floor if she tried.

Claire felt the top of her back connect with a bobbing body. Something was wrong, and not in a way she expected. She tried to open her eyes to see what was happening, but she could barely see outside in the cave. She was completely blind under the water.

Her lungs began to burn as she used up every ounce of oxygen she had in them, still pushing forward and diving down.

Her time was up; Claire needed to breathe. She turned in the direction of the surface. Her arms reached upward and she kicked with all her might.

Thump!

Claire's arm connected with another body, but she pushed through it.

She didn't surface.

The body was below the water with her. Claire reached past it, pushing the corpse aside, and continued upwards.

Thump!

Another body.

And another and another.

Every direction she pushed, she felt squishy skin and heard the deafening *thump* of another corpse in her way. She was in a pool of dead bodies, fighting to reach fresh air. Claire kicked, feeling her bones connect with faces and chests. Soon, she was literally pushing off bodies and using them as a platform to push herself further up towards oxygen.

Finally, she breached the surface and gasped for air. She coughed deep and painfully. After half a minute or so of fighting for air, she managed to calm herself and assess the situation.

"You've got to be fucking kidding me," Claire muttered to herself.

"Claire?!" Tiff screamed in the distance. "I can't see you! Where are you?"

The bodies were gone. There was only an empty pool again of water.

And Claire was back where she started, further from shore.

She felt her body lose hope. As if it had a mind of its own and the electronic signals from her brain seemed to go ignored as her arms and legs deflated, lifeless. As if her arms and legs heard the brain say *we're fucked* and the arms and leg responded with *well then, what's the point?*

Kicking to keep her head above water was proving to be too demanding. Claire was having a hard time keeping her face out of the water.

Then she heard it.

Like a whisper carried on a nonexistent wind through the tunnels of the cave. A deep voice said, "Another body for my collection."

She turned around to locate the voice, only to see a dark figure standing on the water behind her. A tall, lean figure with glowing red eyes. It reached out towards her.

The electronic signals in her brain sent a new message to her body: *get fucking moving.*

And so she did.

Claire pushed her body forward, sending herself faster than she knew was possible. She was weak and tired. Exhausted from everything that had happened to them in the weeks since their trapping in the cave. Now, this. She didn't want to die. She wasn't really too sure of it before this moment, but now she knew for sure.

She wanted to live.

She wanted to see her husband again. Kiss him. Hold him. Love him.

Claire pushed through the water, towards James. He was out there, somewhere, waiting for her.

No, she wasn't doing this for him. Though, Claire loved him so much, this moment wasn't about him. Yes, he was a part of her, just as much as she was a part of him. But he'd left her behind to do some heroic bullshit. Claire was by herself because of him. So now, she wasn't doing this for him.

She was doing this for herself.

Claire pushed through the water. Bubbles began to rise to the surface as they had before. The *thumping* of bodies breaching the surface was immediately overwhelming. Claire's arms connected with bobbing bodies, one after the other. Every inch of the water was being penetrated with rising corpses, but Claire pushed forward.

She could see Tiff again.

Claire pushed through the last body, this time further than she had previously made it.

"Claire!" Tiff screamed, pointing towards her.

Claire felt a hand wrapped around her ankle a second before she was pulled beneath the water. The nails digging into her skin tore the flesh from her bone.

She could feel the metallic taste of blood as it mixed with the water and into her mouth. She screamed, but the sound disappeared in a fury of bubbles.

The nails continued to dig deeper into the meat of her calf. They pierced and pinched, ripped and tore into her leg. The hand climbed further up her leg, shredding the skin as it moved upwards.

Claire continued to scream. The pain of everything was too much. She had fought so hard, but in the end she would become just another body damned to float in the pool.

Something grabbed her wrist and tried pulling her forward.

It felt like the two hands were playing tug-of-war with her as the rope, but the grip on her leg hadn't been prepared for it. The arm above water pulled her free. Claire used her uninjured leg to kick back the attacker and escape.

She gasped for air as she surfaced, doing her best to swim towards the shore, but allowing Tiff to do most of the work. She just needed to breathe.

Claire felt her legs kick rocks below as she neared the edge of the pool. Feeling the ground beneath her was enough incentive for Claire to crawl forward until she was entirely out of the water. She then fell over onto her back as her chest heaved back and forth as she began to laugh.

She had made it.

"Claire!" Tiff screamed.

Something was wrong.

Tiff didn't sound as close as she should have. Claire rolled over to see her running from down the shore towards her.

Claire then rolled over to see who'd pulled her from the water and was now standing over her.

"Hector?" she said weakly.

Hector nodded. "The one and only."

He then turned and walked back into the shadows of the cave.

Sixteen.

Robyn screamed as she was pulled down the dark tunnels.

She tried kicking and squirming; she even reached forward and tried prying herself free.

It wasn't much use.

She reached out and grabbed a large rock that was exposed from the ground, wrapping both hands around it, but it was little use. The skinny, white arms tightened around her chest until she could hear her bones *pop*. Robyn let go of the rock as she once again tried to free herself from the grip.

Blood oozed down her shoulder. She could feel the warm liquid stick to her shirt and mat her hair, mixing with the dirt and grim she'd collected over her short time in the cave.

The figure kept pulling her deeper into the cave, turning as needed. It was also too easy for the figure.

In the back of Robyn's head, she knew this had been a trap. Nothing had worked. They'd been drawn far away from their shelter, and forcefully split up. Taken away from the group so they could be picked apart, one by one.

It didn't mean that she was going to give up.

No, if this was going to be her last stand (and by all accounts, it looked to be that way), she was going to make it a hell of an ordeal for the creature.

For the moment, Robyn rested. She needed to save her energy for when the time was right.

The figure couldn't keep going on forever. It had a plan to take her deeper into the tunnels to something, somewhere.

Robyn relaxed her body and used one of her free hands to put pressure on the wounds along her shoulder. As she waited for what came next, she calmed her breathing. Maintained her focus. She wasn't going to get out of this if she wasn't fully in the moment. Robyn knew that panicking and making rash decisions would lead to her demise.

Finally, the creature came to a stop.

Robyn felt her body soar through the air before she realized that it had heaved her like a rag-doll across a room. She collided with a rocky wall and fell to the ground in a puff of dirt and pebbles. Robyn stood and looked at her opponent.

It was a tall, skinny figure. Its body a dull-white, almost light gray, eyes sunken deep in a pocket of black that stretched across its face. The black outlined its mouth, also smearing across the white in a sinister smile. The fingertips looked like little daggers. They came to a point, inches from where the fingertips should have stopped. Both hands displayed little, black daggers, one of which was bloodsoaked from her attack.

The figure stood tall and straight across the room.

It was only then that she noticed the room had only one way out, which the creature was purposely blocking. The center of the room had a stone slab, shoulder height in size. Several torches lined the wall, giving her the most visibility she had seen in days. She looked around herself and noticed that nothing else was too crazy. The walls were what you'd expect in a cave: cold and jagged with rocks. The roof looked like it was ready to collapse at any minute. Large rocks pressed together so tightly they would only take a small earthquake for them to come crashing down. A dark spot in the middle of the ceiling led Robyn to assume there was a hole, probably her only way out, but it would be an almost impossible squeeze.

"Let me go," Robyn said flatly. It wasn't a very strong demand; she knew it wouldn't drag her all this way to just let her leave.

The white figure tipped its head slightly, raising a single, long finger to its mouth to *shush* her.

Robyn raised her hands and nodded that she understood.

She acted with almost no notice. Robyn wasn't particularly fast, but she was surprised by how fast she could be if she needed to be. She sprinted up to the flat slab in the center of the room, climbing it like it was something she'd done a million times. She didn't have any time to spare—the figure could have already been on her and she only hoped that she'd caught it off guard.

Now on the slab, she stood to look at the hole above her.

She wasn't going to make that jump. It had been a good idea, but now that she was here, it was pointless. She would need a ladder, or at the very least, a decent step stool to get a grip on the hole. That also meant she'd have to pull herself in through the hole, which Robyn now realized wasn't going to happen either.

She looked over to the figure, which hadn't moved. Hadn't

budged.

It knew she wasn't going anywhere.

A small smile crept across its pale face.

"Yeah," Robyn said. "Wouldn't mind giving me a lift, would ya?"

The figure's smile dropped.

The finger raised to its lips again to *shush* her.

Robyn rolled her eyes.

"I'm going to be quiet," Robyn said to the figure. "Not because you told me to…" She looked around the room for anything she could use to get her up through the hole, then finished her sentence in a whisper. "... but because I'm thinking."

Long, black shadows were suddenly cast against the wall, with glowing halos of orange.

Robyn turned back towards the entrance and watched as the white figure stepped aside. A figure wearing a white cloak, with the hood pulled over its head, stepped forward, holding a brilliant lantern.

Behind the cloaked figure was another person, also wearing a cloak. And another. As far back as Robyn could see, a line of people all in matching cloaks were moving in a single line into the room. They wrapped around the slab that Robyn stood on, trapping her within moments.

She tried to gauge the likelihood of her escape now.

The entrance was pointless.

Even if she managed to slip past the tall, white figure with the black smile, she'd be elbow to elbow with the new mass of hooded people.

Her only escape would be through the hole.

A hole she couldn't reach.

None of the hooded people looked up at her. They knew she was there. Expected her to be there. They walked almost quietly on the ground. The only audible sound was a strange *squishing* sound that Robyn couldn't place.

The group circled around her until there was no room left for anyone else.

The figure holding the lantern stood at the top of the slap.

Robyn looked around and realized something she hadn't previously: this wasn't a random slab or rock.

It was flat. Smooth. Almost polished.

It was a large table. An altar!

"Fuck me," Robyn whispered to herself.

The cloaked figure with the lantern lifted it into the air, then slowly placed it at the head of the table. She heard the *clang* of the metal connecting with the stone slab. As if they were waiting for the sound, too, the nearest cloaked person on each side of Robyn grabbed her by the wrists. She tried to pull her arms free. She yanked them upwards and downwards, left to right. She pulled as hard as she could.

Then she saw the hands holding her.

She became dizzy.

Nauseous.

Robyn didn't consider herself to have a weak stomach, but this was almost too much for her.

The hands gripped her wrists tighter. As they readjusted their holds, Robyn focused on them. Their fingers were not white, but a dulled yellow. Dark, symmetrical holes ran the entirety of the hands. Like someone wanted to see what human skin would look like if it was made of honeycomb. Random holes were oozing clear liquid that clung to her own skin, leaving behind a gross, thick goo.

Another figure on each side stepped forward and reached for her ankles. Robyn was quick to kick them away, landing a shoe to the dome of the first one, but within a moment someone else had caught her ankles mid-air.

She squirmed, trying her best to wiggle free, but they were too strong.

The cloaked figures lifted her into the air and softly placed her back on the table.

Robyn screamed.

She didn't even know what she was screaming, but she was doing everything she could to hopefully scare them away. Noises and swears came pouring from her mouth. She threatened them. Begged them. Called them every offensive word her brain could think of (and there were plenty logged inside there).

The cloaked figures didn't retreat. Instead, they continued to pin her down with little effort. Nothing Robyn did could budge her even an inch.

Above her head, she sensed a new movement.

The figure that had held the lantern, picked it back up and slowly raised it over their head again. Then it glided the glow over her body and placed the lantern upon her chest. It then reached over with its hole-filled hands to the wounds along her shoulder.

"What are you doing?" Robyn asked. Her voice raised an octave. "Stop. Stop."

The goo from the holes slowly streamed off the leader's hand and soaked into her shirt, like a clear syrup. It clung to her clothing, its chill penetrating and bracing the skin underneath. The figures grabbed the hole of the shirt and slowly began to pull it back, expanding it from the size of a bottle-cap to a gap large enough to fit a fist.

Her bloodsoaked skin was exposed.

The fingers then left her shirt and hovered above her shoulder wound instead.

"Please stop," Robyn said softly. "Please."

One hand flipped over and exposed its palm. The second hand's thumb and pointer finger made a small pinching motion as it moved towards the other hand. The fingers dug into one of the holes in the center of the palm. It began to overflow with clear liquid that spread over the top of its hand. The fingers dug in, stretching the hole, but not to the point of splitting the skin.

Then, the fingers stopped.

Robyn watched in horror as the fingertips extracted from the hole something black. It was too thick to fit through the hole at first, because the surrounding skin was trying to pull the object back inside. Like the head of a child pressing out of the birthing canal. Eventually, the black object popped free of the suction. The figure's fingertips were raised over Robyn's face to show her what it had for her.

As if it wanted her to see it.

Wanted her to know what it was.

She didn't want to look. Her eyes closed tightly.

The cold goo dripped from the hand and onto her face. She could feel it. It was cold and thick. It had an odor that reminded her of decay. Like walking into a hot room with an open bag of trash that had been forgotten.

Robyn couldn't take it—the goo falling onto her face was bad enough. She had to know what it was from.

Above her face, pinched between two fingers, was a black slug.

It wiggled between the fingers back and forth.

"No," Robyn said softly. "No."

The fingers moved the slug from in front of her face and towards the wound. The second hand then shoved two fingers into her wound and expanded it.

Robyn screamed.

The pain was unimaginable, but she screamed more for what she knew was about to happen.

The fingers moved the slug over her open wound and tucked it away into her bloody tissue.

Robyn screamed again. Screamed like she had never screamed in her life.

Tears streamed down her face and collided with the slug goo that had accumulated on her cheeks. Snot ran down her nostrils and mixed with the saliva from her mouth. She screamed harder than she ever had.

Then the hands moved away from the wound.

One hand flipped over, revealing its palm.

The second hand moved towards a hole that was covered in the slug goo and dug in.

Seventeen.

Doug woke up again.

He smiled and made short jokes through the blood that had pooled inside his mouth.

Tiff knew it was for her. He was trying to calm her. Settle her down. Tiff was grateful that Doug would put her feelings ahead of his own, even with his face wrecked. Any sane person would have understood him needing to take time to process and recover.

But not Doug.

Tiff knew he was dealing with it, but he wouldn't show it. Comedy was his way of processing.

Claire, on the other hand, wasn't about to make any jokes.

The two girls sat beside Doug. The quiet chamber of the cavern filled with heavy breathing and the occasional whimpering. Claire was strong. Stronger than Tiff would have given her credit for, but she wasn't in a good state. Her right leg was pouring blood. From her ankle to inner thigh, there were claw and bite marks. Flaps of meat and flesh dangled over blood and puss. Her leg had swelled the moment she left the water. Tiff had to help move her away from the water's edge. The entire time, Claire had been calling for Hector.

Hector.

Tiff occasionally looked over her shoulder.

He was out there somewhere.

Watching.

Afraid to step out of the shadows.

He occasionally joined them in the safety of their cave they were using as their home. The low light made perfectly dark corners for him to huddle in and disappear from full view. Now that the group had abandoned the home, and hopefully the cave entirely, Tiff wondered if Hector was reeling. He wasn't going with them. Hector would be down here forever.

The thought was too much for her to process. Instead, she leaned forward and wrapped her arms around Claire as she cried silently to herself.

Claire winced as she accidently touched her own leg. "Fuck."

"It'll be alright," Tiff whispered as she rested her head upon Claire's shoulder. "Things could be worse."

Claire wrapped an arm around Tiff's head, cradling it in a makeshift hug.

"Yeah," Doug said weakly. "I'm not trying to be *that guy*, but you kinda rained on my parade here."

Claire laughed.

"I'm just saying, when we get out of here, everyone was going to ask me questions and I was going to get so much male-tail from this... but now I have to share the spotlight with you," Doug said, smiling.

"Maybe..." Claire began as she wiped tears from her face, "... maybe we could do talk show circuits together. You know, 'Today, we have two of the survivors that were stupid enough to get lost in a haunted cave and get fucked up along the way.'"

"Ah," Doug said, "the dream."

The group laughed, and for a fleeting moment, it felt like they weren't in the cave. Instead, they were out hiking in the woods together. Darkness falling upon them, but with it feeling more like a comforting blanket instead of impending doom. They joked and laughed. They did mock interviews about surviving and laughed at each other's expense.

It was a fun break from reality.

"My fucking calf," Claire said. "It hurts so bad."

Tiff looked for herself. There were long, deep cuts running the length of the muscle. It looked like someone had used a can opener on her leg with blades that were dull and rounded. The skin was peeled back and splitting. They had torn a piece of Claire's shirt to make a tourniquet, but still the wounds bled. She'd need medical attention before long. The group would hopefully return soon and find that they weren't lifting one person out, but two. Claire would bleed out if she didn't get help.

"Try not to touch it," Tiff said as she redirected Claire's fingers from her wound. "That'll just make things worse."

"I know," Claire said. "It just hurts. It feels like there are rocks inside my leg."

"Probably," Tiff said. "You probably have dirt and rock embedded inside, but the doctors will take care of that when we get out of here."

Claire nodded. "I know. It's just..." She reached for Tiff's hand and directed it to her wound. "Feel this."

Tiff hadn't expected Claire to put her hand over the wound. .

She pulled her hand away as fast as she could, but not before her fingertips brushed the injury.

Claire was right. Something there was bulging.

Tiff hesitated.

She carefully brought her hand back to the wound. Her fingertips glided over the gaping rip in Claire's leg.

Claire grabbed her hand and guided her to the proper area. "See?"

Tiff closed her eyes and concentrated. She could feel it. Something was under the skin, though not directly under the wound. The wound was an inch or so away from the part of her calf that raised with a little bump. There was something tucked inside her calf.

"What is it?" Tiff asked.

"Right?" Claire said. "It wasn't there minutes ago."

Tiff pulled her hand back and wiped the blood onto her shirt. "Claire, it is probably a rock from me dragging you back. Something lodged itself inside as I clumsily pulled you away from the water. I'm very sorry if it's my fault, but it's just a rock. Any doctor worth their training can get that out for you. We'll be fine."

"Yeah, I know," Claire. "The logical part of my brain knows it's just a rock and the most logical explanation is it just got caught inside my wound. But I have this aching in the back of my head that says it wasn't always there. I remember cleaning the blood off when we first stopped, but I don't remember this bulge being there at the time."

"Of course you don't," Tiff said. "You were kinda in shock, hun."

Claire nodded and continued to roll her finger over the bump.

"Should I get a grill?" Doug said.

"What?" Tiff answered.

"You know, a grill," he reiterated. "Like…" He opened his lips revealing his missing teeth. "A grill."

Claire chuckled. "Like diamonds. You want to know if you should get a diamond grill?"

Doug shrugged. "I don't know. I was thinking of gold. So, I could also dress like a pirate if the opportunity arrived."

The girls laughed.

Doug to the rescue again, lightening the mood.

Tiff smiled and said, "Please, don't get a grill. You don't have enough *cred* to rock a grill."

Doug made a face that showed his displeasure in the answer.

"Strongly disagree."

"Oh, my God," Claire said.

Tiff flung her head towards her.

"I found another one," Claire said. "Here."

Before she'd even finished talking, she had yanked Tiff's hand towards the bottom of the calf.

"Feel that?" she said softly.

Sure enough, Tiff did. It felt slightly smaller than the first, but it was there.

"Oh, fuck," Claire said. "It hurts so fucking much."

"Everything will be alright," Tiff said. "Just try and push it out of your mind."

"No!" Claire screamed as she ran her fingers down her leg. "There's another one near my ankle! This isn't right. This is something else."

"Claire," Tiff said. "Calm down. What else would it be?"

"I don't know," Claire said, beginning to panic. Tears streamed down her face. "I just know they aren't rocks."

Then Tiff saw it.

She watched as something began to form near the highest point of the wound along her thigh. A new bulge suddenly appeared from nothing.

Claire leaned back in pain.

"Feel the first one again," she said.

Tiff reached for the first bump along Claire's calf.

"It feels bigger now, doesn't it?"

Tiff shrugged, trying to hide her own confusion and fear. "I–I don't know."

"I know it. I know it's bigger," Claire groaned.

Corey was hesitant to use his flashlight as he followed the decline. If he was able to keep quiet enough, he might be able to sneak up on the tree-headed figure carrying his wife down the tunnel. If he used his flashlight, he would lose the element of surprise.

But he also knew it was all pointless. The odds of sneaking up on the figure was zero-to-none. This was all designed. All a trap, and he was sprinting in the dark straight towards it.

Corey paused and listened for anything that would tell him he was still behind them. That they hadn't slipped a corner while Corey was pushing blindly through the dark.

Nothing.

The tunnel was quiet.

His thoughts began to drift.

He considered how quickly things had come undone only moments earlier. How fast Robyn, James, and Hali were torn away from him.

His brother was chasing after Robyn. Hopefully he'd be able to find her and they wouldn't be alone. Corey was chasing Hali, and come hell or high water he'd find her, but the same couldn't be said for James.

No one was chasing after him. He was on his own. Again.

Corey hoped that the group lucked upon him later, much like they did the last time. He didn't want to have to explain it to Claire. Tell her that her husband was someplace lost and alone. Dragged away by some evil inside the tunnels.

Corey shook the thought from his head. There wasn't time to dwell on it now. A time would come, probably in the near future, but that wasn't a *now* problem.

Hali was the only thing he needed to focus on. Once she was safe, then he'd have time to think about the next step.

Corey took a step forward and stopped.

His feet were used to the stoney surface of the caves. A familiar discomfort that would probably leave him with lower back problems for the rest of his life. However, for the first time in what felt like forever, he didn't step onto rocks or dirt. Something was different and he could tell with a single step.

Corey debated whether he should continue forward without revealing himself with the flashlight, but knew he didn't have a choice. He pulled out the flashlight and aimed it at his feet.

Click.

The floor illuminated beneath him. The light reflected from a linoleum floor of a large black and white checkered pattern. The white was scuffed and old, but appeared to have been recently cleaned. Like someone mopped it once a week.

Corey raised his flashlight and investigated the rest of the room. The walls were made of dry-wall, not stone, and were painted off-white. There were even pictures hanging in dusty frames, including a lighthouse overlooking a storm. The painting was familiar but he couldn't decide why. Two foldable chairs with discolored cushions sat on both sides of the tunnel.

But wait, it wasn't a tunnel anymore.

It was a hallway.

Corey turned with his flashlight to see it eat away the darkness.

The hallway pushed back deeper into the tunnel than Corey expected.

Chairs and painted pictures lining the walls as far back as he could see.

"Well, fuck," he said to himself.

Another part of the trap.

He'd walked straight into it, just like he thought he would.

Corey took a few cautious steps before realizing that there was no point. The element of surprise had been used against him. He picked up his pace and pressed forward. The hallway wasn't real; it wasn't going to follow any set rules or laws that Corey would expect. The only option was to press forward. He was going to have to see what the cave wanted him to see, so there was no use in fighting it.

Each step made an unpleasant *squeaking* sound that reverberated down the hallway. His tennis shoes left scuffs behind him as he walked. It was an eerie walk. There was no sign of life anywhere. He passed the two foldable chairs and the painting outside the hallway, then saw them all again further ahead, repeated. It was a pattern that would follow him down the hallway as far as he could make out.

He moved, each step faster than the last until he was jogging.

Every time he passed the chairs, he noticed they were becoming more discolored. Their cushions began to rip and fray. The painted metal frames of the chairs began to peel and rust. The dust and grime on the painting's frame also thickened with each pass. Soon enough, the painting itself began to age. The lighthouse rotted as the canvas molded into a mess of brown and green.

Corey paused. He'd heard something in the distance. It had been quiet, but still unmistakable.

He moved forward in its direction as the sound increased from a whisper. Nevertheless, it was still gibberish from this distance.

Then something else changed.

He could see the hallway coming to an end. There was a wall with a push door. On the left side of the door was a small table. To its right, there was something sticking out from the wall.

It all felt familiar in a way that Corey couldn't put his finger on.

He'd seen this all before. The chairs. The black and white floor with scuff marks. The dirty, old painting.

It finally came flooding back to him at the sight of the door.

Corey slowed his jog down and cautiously approached the end of the hall.

The table beside the door had pamphlets. Folded pieces of paper that he knew at one time said "Living in Faith Church" with a picture of Jesus holding out his hands. Now the pages were so aged and faded that only the faintest ghost of an outline could be seen.

Beside the pamphlets was a gold cross that had been knocked over, covered in cobwebs and dust. To the right of the door, hanging off the wall was a little bowl. The same bowl that Corey would dip a finger in and with holy water perform the sign of the cross. Now, it was full of dry dirt.

Corey placed a hand on the door, readying himself to push it forward. He knew what he expected on the other side. A room full of foldable chairs placed in a circle. A table on the far side with old donuts and older coffee. A room he used to frequent when his father first passed away. A support group for people that had lost loved ones. It'd helped him move forward instead of going down a dark path.

He hadn't thought about the group in years. Simply driving by the church did nothing but spark memories of the dark hole he was trying to crawl out of while in the support group. Sure, they had ultimately helped him, but now that he was out... the sight of the church was unpleasant and made his head hurt.

He pushed open the door.

It was exactly as he remembered it.

Even down to the full lightbulbs that hung on dusty chandeliers from the ceiling. The smell of cigarettes and coffee flooded his nostrils.

However, the one thing he wasn't expecting was for the chairs to be occupied. In unison, the individuals in the chairs slowly turned their heads towards Corey at the doorway.

The lights inside the room flickered off.

And the door behind him slammed.

Eighteen.

Bird waited, tucked away in the tunnel.

He had chased after Robyn, knowing the general direction she had been swept away, but when he almost gave up hope, he noticed the blood.

Blood from Roybn's shoulder from the attack.

He followed its crimson trail, sprinting at times, only slowing to refocus on its direction as the blood turned various corners.

Bird pushed through the dark tunnels as fast as he could until he knew where she was.

He was moving so fast, all the while focused on the ground looking for the next splatter of blood, that he almost ran into a line of cloaked figures. They stood shoulder to shoulder, engulfing the entire width of the tunnel. They were still, and looking down. Their feet were shredded and bloody. It looked like they were walking on ground beef.

Bird now wondered if it was their blood or Robyn's that he had been following.

But it didn't matter. They were hovering around something, and with this being the general direction that Robyn disappeared, Bird was willing to bet it all that she was the focus of their attention.

Then he heard screams echoing from ahead.

It was Robyn screaming in pain and horror. Something was happening to her, something wicked and awful, but there was nothing that Bird could do to help.

Be strong, Rob, he thought to himself as he slowly moved into the shadows of a corner. *You gotta make it through this, I'm so fucking close. Please.*

He waited in the corner for what felt like an eternity, listening to the screams of one of his best friends. Unable to help her. Her screams echoed down the dark tunnels, replacing one after another.

But there was more than just screams. There were also insults and jabs at whoever was with her. They came so unexpected that Bird had to stop himself from actually laughing out loud.

However, like all things, it finally stopped.

For a moment, Bird feared the worst. That the torture, the pain she was suffering, whatever it was, had taken her.

"Fuck you, you fucking coward with your bitch-ass hoodie!" Robyn screamed.

And in one swift motion, without any indication (or, at least, none that Bird had seen), the cloaked figures turned to march back down the tunnels.

Bird waited for them to leave, but the line seemed to stretch endlessly. Figure after figure walked by him. They moved exactly the same. Each figure was hooded and looking toward the ground, their hands clenched together at their chest, draped in large sleeves, their feet raw and bloody from walking so long in unison. Bird watched until the final figure finally passed. This one was identical to the rest, except for an obnoxious lantern they were holding out in front of them. Once the hooded figures left, the figure that snatched her away from the group followed.

They were done with Robyn. Whatever their goal, they had accomplished it.

Bird watched as the figures disappeared into the shadows, waiting for the coast to be clear. Even then, he listened for the sound of bloody feet against rock to fade.

Only once he was sure he was alone in the tunnel did he leave the safety of his hiding place. Bird bounded out of the shadows and sprinted towards the corner from which the figures had emerged.

There, he found Robyn, curled in a ball atop a large stone slab and crying.

"Rob?" Bird said softly to not alarm her.

She looked up at him as he cautiously stepped forward. Her eyes were large and wet. Tears ran down her face in uninterrupted streams. It was a constant flood of water that came from her eyes, as if a faucet behind her eyes had been left on.

She reached out for him and Bird grabbed her, holding her close to his chest, and let her cry.

As Bird held her close, he could have sworn he felt something wiggle against his chest.

Claire was right.

There was something under her skin.

Tiff felt it. Whatever it was had a rock-like quality to it. Hard. Sharp. But rocks don't simply grow and appear out of nowhere. Though everything in the logical part of her brain told her that none of this made sense, the part of her brain that had registered everything unexplainable won out. She didn't need to listen to reason; actually, quite the opposite. She *couldn't* listen to reason. Reason and expectations would get them killed.

Something was under Claire's skin, something that wasn't there moments ago.

"I need to get it out!" Claire screamed.

Tiff reached out for her hand, stopping her. "Wait, let's just talk about this for a moment."

She felt Doug's hand rise from the ground beside her. As unexpected as it was, it also felt reassuring and comforting. "Don't," he said.

Her comfort immediately dissipated. "What?"

"Don't," Doug repeated as he took her hand away from Claire. "This isn't your call. She is going through this and we need to just support her."

Tiff glared at her cousin. Even with his face bruised and broken, and his lips gashed and teeth missing, he held some kind of authority with his look. He gave her a slight smile and said, "It's going to be okay."

"Nothing's *okay*," Tiff said. The squeak in her voice let her know she was barely holding in to her emotions. She was a loose button threatening to snap from a blouse.

"We can't control that," Doug said. "But this—what she does next—she can control."

And with that, Tiff slowly released Claire's hand.

Claire looked from Doug to Tiff, as if she was asking permission with her eyes. Asking for it to be the right move, hoping for an answer.

No answer was going to come.

There was no *right* move.

Only *moves*.

Claire looked down to her knee and began to pinch at one of the mounds. She winced in pain as she rolled around the object under her skin. A sharp "ah-ah" left her lips as she got a grip and began to slide the mound towards the wound on her knee.

Tiff watched the mound slide under the skin of her friend. It moved slowly and with hesitation. She felt the sudden urge to throw up. She wasn't usually a squeamish person, but the strange sight of Claire sliding the little object under her skin was enough to make her one.

Claire stopped. She winced in pain again and said, "I-I can't slide it any more."

Tiff felt relief flood over her as she placed a hand on Claire's shoulder. "That's fine. That's okay."

Claire flicked her hand off her shoulder. "No, it's not."

Claire released the object. She hovered her fingers above the wound on her knee for a moment.

"Don't," Tiff begged.

"I have to," Claire said as she carefully dug two fingers into the wound.

Tiff turned her head away. She couldn't watch. The sound was bad enough.

Claire opened her mouth and let out a piercing scream. The violence of it made Tiff cover her ears.

Tiff looked down at Doug, who hadn't turned away. He winced as he watched the scene unfold in front of him. Eventually, he gave up and lowered his eyes entirely.

Finally, the screaming stopped.

Hesitantly, Tiff uncovered her ears and turned towards Claire.

"I think it's almost out," Claire said softly.

Claire removed her fingers from the wound. They were covered in blood up to the first knuckle.

The mound was there now. Just barely hidden behind the flesh. Tucked away inside the open wound that was now bleeding profusely from Claire diggering her fingers inside it and stretching the frayed skin.

Claire put her thumb on the opposite side of the mound and pushed it out.

Tiff watched in horror as something flung out of the wound and onto the dirt floor.

Claire reached down and grabbed it, pinching it between her thumb and finger.

Though covered in blood, it almost looked like an ice cube. The blood was somehow translucent in some areas, with the beam of their flashlight shining cleanly through it.

"Oh, my God," Claire said. "It's glass."

"No, it's not," Tiff said as she reached out her hand and waited for Claire to pass it over. But she didn't. Claire dropped the object to the dirt floor and began to dig at her ankle instead.

"There's more," Claire declared. "I can feel them forming."

"Stop it," Tiff said as she picked up the bloody object from the ground. "You are going to hur–"

She looked at the object in her hand.

The small, bloody object was unmistakable. Claire wasn't overreacting. What Tiff held in her hand was a chunk of glass.

Tiff waited for the words to form, much like the glass that was growing under Claire's skin, but found none as she watched a small mound beside Claire's ankle grow the size of a marble.

Claire howled as she pushed the bump around her bone and popped it out of her wound. Tiff could hear the ripping and tearing of meat as Claire pushed it tightly under the skin. Blood streamed out as fresh lines were cut under her skin.

Tiff reached out to hold Claire's hand as she moved from her ankle back to her knee. "Stop," she whispered.

Claire looked back at her. Tiff could see everything Claire was feeling in her swollen eyes. The confusion. The pain. The fear.

"Why is this happening?" Claire asked as the tears fell. She launched herself towards Tiff, tucking in her body for a hug and allowing Tiff to wrap her small arms around her. She bounced up and down as she tried to catch her breath through the tears.

Tiff held her as tightly as she could in her arms.

"I don't know," Tiff said. "I don't know why any of this is happening, but I can promise you that when we get out of here, it will be gone. This isn't going to continue outside of this hellhole. We are going to walk out of here and everything will go back to normal."

"How can things go back to normal?" Claire asked as she pulled away. "Things will never be normal again."

Tiff thought about it for a moment. She wasn't wrong. Even if they left and the glass under Claire's skin disappeared, the scars would still be there. Physically and emotionally, they would still be there. Their group would be changed forever. Tiff searched for the right words, struggling for anything that would carry the weight she desired.

Eventually, she settled on: "We will find a new normal, and we will be stronger because of it."

Claire smiled and wiped a tear from her face. She shook her head slowly as she wiped her hand under her nose. "Yeah."

The moment felt good.

Even if there was an overwhelming amount of struggling in their future—something that in her heart, Tiff knew was coming—she took this moment in and was thankful for it.

As if something in the cave could sense their growing calm and wanted to shatter it, Tiff's ears perked up at the sound of movement in the distance.

"What is it?" Claire asked. She'd caught onto the sudden realization flushed over Tiff's face.

She didn't answer right away. Instead, she tried to focus her concentration on the sound. Trying to pinpoint it. Locate the faint sound within the expansive cavern surrounding them.

Tiff heard it again.

It sounded like rocks kicking together. It was someone walking the trail, approaching their location.

"Someone's coming!" Tiff said, having a hard time hiding the excitement in her voice. Even though she said *someone's coming,* her wavering voice and excited tempo easily suggested *the group is back.*

She pointed the flashlight up the trail to where she thought the noise was coming from. Halfway up the trail, she saw a lone figure.

It wasn't what she was expecting. It wasn't the group coming back to them; or, at the very least, it wasn't their entire group.

Tiff saw Claire turn to look at the figure in the light. "Why are they walking away from us?"

It was hard to see. Tiff squinted on the figure in the distance.

It was a large…man?

As she focused on the shape, Tiff saw what Claire saw.

"He is walking away," Tiff confirmed. She watched as the pieces slowly came together for her.

"Wait," she whispered. Tiff lowered the flashlight to her side and looked around. Light bounced off the dirt floor and the small pool of blood that had formed a thick, reddish-brown paste. "Where is Doug?"

"He was right here," Claire said.

Tiff raised her flashlight back up the trail.

It was him.

Her cousin was the figure walking away from them.

"Doug!" Tiff screamed.

She opened her mouth to scream again, but before she could, she saw movement from the corner of her eye.

A thin, white hand appeared on Claire's shoulder.

The flashlight in her hand quivered without her knowing. The light bobbled as if it were on a faultline.

And from the darkness, a face pushed forward from behind her. A white face with no eyes, no nose, no ears. A wrinkled face with no expressions, just a mouth without lips. The face whispered into Claire's ear.

The face then pointed towards Tiff and smiled.

Nineteen.

"Hello everyone," Corey said to the group sitting in the folded chairs before him.

They didn't respond.

"Seems like an awful place to have one of these meetings," Corey said.

He reached behind him and tried to turn the knob to the door.

"Worth a shot," he said as it failed to open. "Listen, I know that you know that I know that this isn't real. Right? Does that make sense?"

The group didn't say anything.

"So, could we just go ahead and move this along? I really don't have the time or the energy for–" he said, waving his hands around, "– whatever this is."

Corey recognized the faces staring back at him.

The members of the group were the same members from the support group he had visited for over a year once his father passed away.

However, the girl at the front, the red-headed lady that usually led the group before, shouldn't have been there; she had died a year ago, hit by a car..

Marla sat in the metal chair and placed a hand onto the single empty chair beside her, patting it. Inviting him over.

"Gonna have to give that a pass, Marla," Corey said.

He walked around the outside of the room, past the table with the coffee and assortment of cookies. The cookies were moldy. Green dots speckled in chunks over the otherwise fresh-looking cookies. The smell of mold and decay filled his nostrils. Corey pushed past it towards the exit that was *usually* located in the back.

Two men stood from their chairs and watched Corey walk around the room.

"David, Rob," Corey said, acknowledging them. "Nice to see you two."

The men were always funny to see together back when Corey was a regular. David was a shorter man with a chip on his shoulder. Always something to say, even if the thing he had to say was unnecessary and sometimes rude. However, he was there when you needed him, and Corey definitely needed him at times. In stark contrast, Rob was a towering figure. His hair was thin from his balding. He looked like he could easily plug and play as a stuntman on *Game of Thrones*. He was quieter. Sadder than most in the group. Due to the little experience he'd had with the group, Rob hadn't made a single step towards recovering from his loss.

Corey could always relate. He understood both men.

"I'm just gonna move on, guys," Corey said. "I know you aren't real, and I'm still confident I could outrun both of you if I need to."

The men watched Corey as he moved around the group and towards the back of the room. They didn't follow him with more than the rotation of their heads.

He found the exit just as it was in real life, tucked behind a red curtain in the back of the room. Corey pulled the curtain aside and grabbed the handle.

He twisted.

The door refused to open.

"Yeah," Corey said with a nod of his head. "That seems about right."

He turned to reassess his options, only to find himself standing face to face with Rob and David.

"Quicker than I remember," Corey said. He nervously laughed at his own joke as the men didn't budge. Their faces remained hard and motionless.

Corey sprang to his left, hoping to catch them off guard, but failed.

Rob and David collapsed upon him. Rob used his large hands to grip Corey's bicep and overpower him, dragging him towards the group. David used both hands to wrap around Corey's arm. Though it wasn't as threatening, the implication was clear.

Corey looked down at David. "I appreciate the effort, but I think Rob is more than enough."

The two men pulled Corey towards the empty seat and sat him down.

Corey didn't argue. He didn't have much of a choice, it appeared. He sat down and pulled his arms free from the grip of the two men, who remained standing behind him. A shadow that Corey knew wouldn't let him leave. Instead, Corey crossed his arms and placed one leg over his knee. "Okay then," he said. "Let's fucking get this going."

Marla looked at Corey for longer than someone should ever blankly stare at another person. It wasn't only uncomfortable, but it continued until his skin filled with goosebumps. Corey opened his mouth to ask her to stop, but before he could do so, she slowly rotated her head towards the group.

Corey followed her gaze.

The group was full of familiar faces except for one.

A single man was out of place. And he looked back at Corey expressionless.

"Hello, father," Corey said.

Robyn peeled away from Bird and thanked him. She wiped what tears were left on her face with the backside of her hand and smiled.

"What happened?" Bird asked.

Robyn shook her head. "Doesn't matter."

She could feel it, squirming around under her skin.

The slugs that were plugged into the wound on her shoulder.

They crawled, slowly, under her flesh and she could feel them. However much it hurt, Robyn knew there was nothing good that could come from talking about it. Bird would only stress and freak out about something that he couldn't help.

Instead, she tried not to think about the squirming under her skin, and instead focused on what she could control.

Which, unfortunately, wasn't much down here.

"What happened to everyone else?" Robyn asked as she rolled off the slab and put her feet on the ground.

"Don't know," Bird replied. "Corey and I split up after you and Hali."

"And James?" Robyn asked.

Bird shrugged. "Don't know."

"So," Robyn said, "the cave split us up."

"Seems that way."

"Where do we go from here?" Robyn asked.

Again, Bird shrugged.

Robyn walked towards the only exit from the room. She stepped over dirt and rocks covered in blood left behind by the barefooted group. There was the smell of fresh blood lingering in the air.

Movement in Robyn's shoulder caused her an involuntary spasm. She swatted at her chest instinctively. The thought of crushing a slug under her skin made her want to vomit. Was it worse to have them alive and crawling through her body, or to have them splattered and dead under her skin?

Click, click, click.

A sound echoed down the dark tunnels.

Something was coming.

Click, click, click.

"For fuck's sake," Robyn said. "Just give us some fucking time to gather ourselves, please."

The sound grew louder in the dark tunnels, causing Robyn to step back into the small room with the stony slab at its center. She stepped backwards with Bird and listened as the sound continued to grow.

Click, click, click.

"What do you think it is?" Robyn whispered.

"No idea," Bird said. "Ten dollars says it's something I hate and is a thing that would crawl out of my nightmares."

Robyn smirked. "Not taking that bet."

The sound stopped.

A wave of dread filled the room.

It was now at the edge of the tunnel, whatever had made the sound. It seemed to be waiting for the right moment to enter the room.

"Oh, come on." Robyn rolled her eyes in frustration. "Get the show fucking going already!"

Something long, black, and pointy entered the room from the edge of the entrance. Then, on the other side, two identical things appeared. Then two more.

"Cool," Bird said. "That's unexpected."

Robyn realized then what she was looking at. These were the legs of a giant spider. There were eight of them, four on each side of the entrance, gripping the corners. They were pitch black with milky white joints. Long, brown hairs covered the legs, making them look sharp.

For a second, the legs relaxed. Then they suddenly sprung back to life, pulling forth a giant body.

The spider was large enough that Robyn couldn't help but hold her breath as it entered the room. Thick, hairy fangs pulsated from the front of the spider's face. A long string of saliva dripped from them as they moved like little hands attached to the spider's face.

And just as fast as the creature had arrived, it pulled itself back into the shadows.

Neither Robyn nor Bird moved.

They remained still, holding their breath.

"Do you think it didn't see us?" Bird whispered.

Robyn brought a single finger to her mouth, hoping that the action was enough for him to realize he needed to shut up.

They stood at the edge of the room, backs pressed against the rocky surface, waiting for something to happen because, of course, it wasn't over. They knew it. They had faced enough, survived enough. Something was about to happen.

Robyn could feel it in her bones, and judging by Bird's tense body, he could feel it, too.

"Do you hear that?" Bird asked.

She did.

There was a cracking sound emitting from outside the entrance, where the spider was waiting.

It was soft and small, but it was there.

"Okay," Bird said. "This is just annoying."

Robyn looked around the room for something to pop out of the entrance or the shadows beside her. Then she remembered something. The room had a hole in the ceiling. It was too far away for her to get out herself, but with Bird here, it might be enough.

"Come on!" she said quietly, but still assertive. She grabbed Bird's hand and moved him to the center of the room. Robyn crawled on top of the rocky slab with visions of what had just occurred minutes ago flooding her mind. The fingers flexing open her wound, placing thick, bloody slugs into her body. She shivered as she recalled the moment, and then did her best to push it away.

She stood directly under the hole in the ceiling and pointed up.

In the entrance, the cracking sound continued.

"Look," Robyn said. "I'll climb up and hopefully out, then I'll reach down and pull you up."

Bird looked up at the hole and then back at Robyn. "Do you think you can lift me?"

"Dude, you are scrawny as fuck," she said. "Yes, I think I can lift you. Now hurry, turn into a table."

Bird rolled his eyes. "Could try saying *please*, at least." He got down on all fours and made a flat surface for Robyn.

She smirked as she carefully stepped on her friend's back. "Please *and* thank you."

Bird said something; however, it was lost in the sound of cracking. It was louder now. Not closer, but obviously louder.

Robyn reached up and was able to grab the edge to the hole that had eluded her earlier.

"Okay," Robyn said. "I've got a grip."

Bird obviously knew what to do next, because he slowly started to stand. He reached his arms around his back and tried to help balance her as he came to a full stance. Robyn had climbed his back until she was standing squarely on his shoulders.

She was able to pull her elbows outside the hole now.

"Wait," she heard Bird say from below.

Robyn looked ahead into the darkness of the space she'd climbed into. "What?"

"The sound stopped," Bird said.

Robyn listened for the sound, but it was gone.

"This is really going to suck," she heard Bird say below her.

Robyn felt her body fling against the hole's edge. She lost her grip as her elbows were rocked by the sudden slamming of her body. She slipped backwards through the hole and back into the room.

She felt Bird collapse from under her. She looked down to see him fallen from the slab and swatting at himself violently.

The ground was moving below her. Like the rippling of a lake, the floor moved from the entrance of the room and covered the entirety of the ground.

Bird continued to violently swat at himself, as something dark attempted to swallow his body. Slowly, from his feet up, his body was being ingulfed in something that Robyn couldn't fully see.

Spiders.

Robyn knew it without being able to see them clearly.

There were millions and millions of small spiders covering Bird.

The giant spider from before had laid eggs outside the entrance. The cracking they'd heard was the sound of millions of small spiders bursting free of their eggs. The ground was covered in a wave of them.

"Get the fuck out of here!" Bird screamed as the black mass slowly overtook his entire leg and began to spread over his torso.

Robyn didn't move, not right away. She froze. Watching one of her best friends overrun by millions of spiders. Her body didn't want to move. She couldn't.

"Go!" he screamed.

Robyn snapped out of her daze and tried to pull her body back up through the hole. But she couldn't, because there was nothing left to anchor herself to.

She looked down at her friend and saw that the black mass now covered his chest and was crawling up his shoulders and neck. Robyn could hear the millions upon millions of little legs scrambling across the ground below. Over the dirt and over the rock slab below her feet. She could hear something wet and spongy. She couldn't see what was making the sound, but she knew what it was.

It was the vile sound of a million little fangs ripping into Bird's body.

She felt her hand slipping from its grip on the hole. Robyn looked down at the rocky slab below and knew that she would be swarmed within moments if she couldn't quickly pull herself out of the room.

She was afraid.

Robyn could do nothing but watch as Bird was eaten alive by millions of spiders, all the while swatting at his body and trying his best not to succumb to what was inevitable.

She couldn't save him, nor could she save herself.

Robyn felt her grip loosen further. She was mere seconds away from falling.

She looked down at her friend again, and watched him squirm and swat at himself.

"Go!" he screamed. Bird looked up at her, seeing that she was hanging on by a thread.

Bird slowly walked towards her.

Inch by inch.

Blood dripped from his body as he moved. Now that he was closer, Robyn could clearly see the real damage caused by the millions of little fangs. Chunks of meat and clots of blood riddled Bird's body.

Nevertheless, Bird slowly crawled onto the slab and, in doing so, used his hands as leverage to pull up his body.

Which meant that more spiders were able to swarm his arms and up towards his neck.

Robyn watched as they filled his entire body, forcing him down to the rocky surface below.

Bird disappeared beneath the blanket of spiders, reducing him to a black mass upon the floor.

"Bird!" Robyn screamed.

With a sudden burst of energy, Bird flung himself from the sea of spiders below. He shot forward and pushed Robyn upward with the last bit of energy he had remaining.

Robyn climbed up through the hole and landed on her stomach beside the edge. She quickly pulled her legs the rest of the way and rotated her body towards the hole to reach down with an open hand for Bird.

But he was gone.

Robyn watched as the spiders overran everything below, with Bird buried somewhere beneath the chaos.

"No," Robyn said.

She pulled away from the hole and cried. She wasn't normally a crier. It just wasn't something she did in her day to day life. Back at home, Tyler was more likely to cry in the house. She was the one that was emotionally in control at all times. She didn't cry... and that was a source of pride.

However, that didn't matter down here.

In the caves, she'd cried more than she had her entire life.

One of her best friends...no, Bird was more than that. He was *more* than a best friend. Bird was Bird. A man that had always been there for her when Tyler was being annoying. When she was younger and needed a shoulder to cry on or an ear to vent into. He didn't have a mean bone in his body, and never did he make her feel small or unaccepted.

Bird was gone.

And Robyn wasn't prepared to handle it.

A hand reached out and grabbed her shoulder.

She turned around, ready for anything, and threw a punch.

"Oh, fuck," a familiar voice said.

Robyn rubbed the tears from her eyes so that she could focus her sight in the darkness.

She threw herself into the open arms of her husband.

Twenty.

Tiff watched as Claire stood and began to walk towards the trail, joining Doug near the top of the cavern.

The flashlight in her hand bobbled as she closed her eyes and waited for what would inevitably happen to her. Whatever that was that whispered in her friend's ear, telling her to move despite every inch of her body being covered in cuts and with glass in her joints. To move up towards the top of the cavern for an unknown reason.

Tiff felt a hand press against her shoulder.

It was stiff and cold. Even through her shirt, she could feel the cold radiate from the hand. She could feel something beside her ear, breathing.

She closed her eyes tighter and waited to join them on the march up the trail and off down a tunnel to who-knows-where.

"Fuck this," Tiff said as she threw her head to the side, colliding it with the face that she knew had no eyes, ears, or nose. She felt the cold hand drop from her shoulder.

Tiff rolled and began throwing punch after punch at the creature below her. She used her flashlight to swing with as much force as she could at the creature. The sound of cracking bones against a metal flashlight echoed through the cavern.

Tiff didn't stop.

She continued to throw blow after blow with the flashlight until she saw that the flashlight—her only source of light—was dimming. She placed it on the ground and felt around for a rock, eventually finding one the size of a softball. Tiff raised it over her head and brought it down.

She brought the rock up and down so many times that she felt the muscles in her arms burn. When she finally dropped the rock to the ground, the figure was nothing but a pool of blood, bone fragments, and crushed meat. Tiff was covered in a splatter of blood and brain.

Tiff thought about it for a moment, wondering why a ghost would have blood... but pushed the thought from her head. It wasn't important.

She grabbed the flashlight from the ground and raced towards the trail.

Tiff needed to get to her cousin. She couldn't see him as she raced. Whatever time had passed from when she first saw him walking away to beating the fuck out of the whisperer was enough for Doug to possibly walk all the way out of the cavern and maybe down a tunnel. If that was the case, she might never see him again. There was no way to know where he was if that happened. She could only hope that he wasn't out yet.

She saw a figure in front of her.

Claire.

Tiff slowed down for a moment, considering what she could do to help. However, Tiff was fairly certain they were going to the same place, so if she could race ahead and find Doug, then she could hopefully stop him and together they could go back and help Claire.

The logic was barely there. It was just all she could think of to justify her need to find Doug.

She pressed forward. The rocks below her feet slid and skidded away, almost enough for her to slip off the edge and fall to the rocky surface below. Maybe if she was lucky, she could fall into the water instead, but that seemed less and likely as they climbed the trail.

She pointed her flashlight over the edge to view the ground below. She saw large boulders that edged the entire ground, as well as the small hole they would crawl into for sleep. The water took up a majority of the ground below, with bodies floating in the pool by the hundreds. Around them, a long figure walked over the surface of the water.

Then Tiff spotted Hector, standing right where she last saw him helping Claire out of the water. He was looking up at her on the trail. He slowly raised a hand and pointed ahead of her. In Tiff's head, she somehow heard his voice. He said, "Go, before it's too late.".

It took a moment for her to understand, but she did exactly what Hector said. She turned and ran up the trail.

Tiff moved as fast as she could, slipping occasionally on the rocks and dirt, but she regained her balance and continued forward.

Doug was a big man with a long stride. He would easily outwalk her when they were together. Every one step of his was equivalent to two or three of her own. However, even with that fact, he was walking and she was sprinting as fast as she could. Tiff wasn't the most athletic person in the world, but she was surprising herself with just how fast she was able to move up the hill. It was like she was one of those crazy chicks who loved running up mountains in a tank top, yoga pants, and a sweatshirt tied around their waist.

She moved with a fire under her ass, because she was desperate to find her cousin.

The trail leveled out, and Tiff knew this meant they were almost halfway up the trail. It would wrap around the cavern like a catwalk until, twenty yards further, it would continue up and eventually out.

Tiff almost dropped her flashlight at the sight of Doug standing at the point where the trail began to climb once more.

She had done it. She had actually caught up to him.

However, he wasn't walking away. He was standing at the edge of the trail, looking forward towards the emptiness of the cavern.

"Doug!" she screamed as she continued forward, no longer sprinting. She didn't want to spring up on him and cause him to slip off the edge. Tiff moved cautiously. "Doug, let's go."

He didn't answer.

Instead, he inched closer to the edge of the trail.

Rocks were kicked off the trail and down into the pit below. Tiff heard them *click* and *clack* as they landed on the boulders below.

She reached a hand out towards her cousin. "Doug, honey, it's me. Let's get out of this place. We aren't safe here anymore."

Doug didn't respond.

Another inch closer, the toes of his shoes now dangling off the cliff.

Fuck caution. Tiff, now standing close enough to Doug, threw herself forward and pounced her cousin. She grabbed both his arms and tried to keep him from falling.

"Please, Doug, please," she pleaded. She could feel her heart racing out of control. She was breathing fast as she tried to understand what she could do.

She couldn't do this by herself. She wasn't strong enough to hold Doug back.

However, with Claire's help, maybe she could.

Tiff looked back down the trail and spied Claire marching forward.

"Claire, snap out of it! I need you!" she screamed. The words shot out of her mouth with phlegm and snot from her nose as she sobbed. Tiff struggled to keep her grip on her cousin.

Tiff was desperate. It was illogical to assume that Claire was doing anything besides joining her cousin attempting to walk off the cliff.

Something stepped out of the shadows and pushed Tiff aside.

She flew from her cousin and scrambled to get back to him.

Tiff froze at the sight of Doug being held by James.

"Oh, thank you, God," Tiff screamed as she slowly stood and tried to regain her breath. "Thank you, so much. I am so fucking happy to see you."

James pulled Doug slowly away from the ledge, gritting with exertion. Doug was larger, and probably could pull James with him into the pit if he wanted to. The fact that he was moving backwards was a good sign, as far as Tiff was concerned. It meant that Doug didn't really want to step over the edge. It was some kind of unknowing motion that the whisperer had put into action.

"Where's Claire?" James asked as he struggled to pry Doug away.

Tiff looked around, picking up the flashlight from the ground that she'd dropped while struggling with Doug. She aimed it down the trail in search of Claire, who was slowly marching towards them. She was maybe fifty yards away now.

James looked at Tiff and smiled. "Thank you." He looked back at Doug as he pulled him backwards from the ledge. "Come, grab one of his arms. We need to do this together."

Tiff sprang forward. "Of course!"

She stood beside James and grabbed Doug's right arm. She could feel Doug slowly being pulled backwards, away from the cliff.

Tiff's heart picked up again; not out of fear this time, but out of relief. Out of hope.

James leaned over towards her. "You have a good grip, right?"

Tiff adjusted her fingers and said, "I think so."

"Good." James released Doug, leaving her to hold him in place.

"Wait," Tiff said. "Wait, we need to do this together."

James leaned toward her ear again and whispered, "I can't wait to hear the sound of your cousin *splattering* on the rocks below."

"Wha–?" Tiff tried to say, but stopped as she felt Doug inch forward. "No, no, please, James. James, please."

James chuckled and waved. "Good luck."

He turned, picked the flashlight up from the ground, and walked away.

"Stop! Please!" Tiff screamed. She turned back towards her cousin, seeing that they were only several feet from the edge.

Tiff grunted and used both her arms on Doug's right arm to pull him backwards. She pulled and pulled and pulled.

"Tiff," a small voice said from in front of her.

"Doug!?" Tiff screamed.

"Tiff," Doug repeated. "I can't stop."

"Doug! You have to!"

"I can't, it won't let me. I have no control over this. You have to let go before I take us both down," Doug said softly.

"No," Tiff said. "No, that's not an option. I'm not quitting."

"It's not quitting. It's the truth. You aren't strong enough to pull me back, and it's only a matter of time," Doug said.

She felt him inch closer to the edge.

Tiff looked over into the pit by accident. She felt the rush of vertigo, of falling through the air. Her brain screamed at her that she was going over, that she was about to plunge towards death.

"Please," Tiff said as she snapped out of it. "Please Doug, I don't want to do this without you."

"I know," Doug said. "I just don't want to die knowing you gave up."

Tiff felt the tears roll down her face.

"Please, don't give up," Doug said. "You need to survive. Get the fuck out of here."

"How?" Tiff asked.

"I don't know," Doug admitted. "I just believe for some reason that you can."

"Doug," Tiff said softly.

"Let me go," he said.

She continued to pull her cousin's arms for a moment longer before falling to the rocky floor beneath her feet. Tiff pushed her face into her hands as she sobbed.

She heard his feet skid over the dirt and rocks, closer to the edge. He was almost there.

Tiff released her face and looked over to her cousin. "I love you, dude."

Doug paused at the edge, "I love you more, dude."

Then he raised a foot and stepped over the edge, his body following. He leaned forward and was gone.

It happened so fast.

One moment he was there, the next he was swallowed by darkness, taken away from her.

Tiff closed her eyes and plugged her ears. But it wasn't enough. She couldn't escape the *wet-thud* sound that echoed as Doug slammed against the ground below.

Through swollen eyes and tears, Tiff crawled towards the edge. She had to see it.

Had to know he was gone. Had to see it for herself.

Her silent crying turned into loud screaming as her eyes locked onto the blood splattered remains of her cousin on top of a large boulder below.

"Doug!" she screamed.

The sight was horrible.

He was gone.

She was truly by herself.

Then she saw movement below.

Hector was leaving the shadows she had last seen him. He slowly walked around the edge of the water as she sobbed.

A voice sounded in her head once more. "I'm so sorry, Tiffany."

Hector continued around the body of water and towards the giant boulders. He carefully climbed around and over them until he was standing over the lifeless body of her cousin. He looked up at her.

"I want you to know that this isn't what I wanted," he said.

He reached down and grabbed Doug's hand. He lifted him like a friend lifting another friend from the ground who had merely tripped. However, as Doug stood, he peeled off from his dead body like a sticker from its paper backing.

Together, Hector and Doug stared up at her.

Hector's voice, for a final time, entered her head. "I'll take care of him. Now run!"

Twenty-One.

"I see you've got that *spooky* staring thing going pretty well," Corey said to his father. "Very cool."

Corey wasn't an idiot.

He knew that behind him wasn't David or Rob. Beside him wasn't Marla. And, most importantly, in front of him wasn't his father.

"Kid, shut the fuck up," his father said.

"Oh, well, you've gotten his favorite sentence down," Corey said as he gave a small applause to mock whatever this fake-father-thing was.

"You are such a fucking waste," his father said. He stood and walked towards Corey. As he moved, everyone's head swiveled to follow his father. "You are pathetic."

"I feel like the apple doesn't fall far from the tree," Corey said. "I mean, not *your* tree… I don't know where your tree is. My dad's tree is what I'm talking about." He leaned back towards David and said, "I feel like I'm not making sense again. I get my words all messed together when I get nervous. And I get real nervous when I'm sitting in front of a group of assholes."

Corey was pulled forward, his father grasping onto the collar of his shirt with his left hand. "Hey, lay off the shi–"

A powerful punch collided with his face, smashing his glasses in the process.

Corey felt his eye socket fracture.

He knew how to take a punch or two. If his real dad had taught him anything, it was how to take a beating. He wasn't the most nurturing person. In fact, his passing was kind of a relief. Corey no longer had to live under his thumb, the same thumb that threatened to squash him like a bug. Though Corey loved his father, sometimes he wondered if it was because he didn't actually know what love was before meeting Hali. After she came along, everything he thought he understood about love was changed. He didn't *love* his father. He *feared* him. He loved him in the sense that up until that moment—the moment that he realized how much he loved his wife all those years ago—he thought that with love came pain. Whether it was physical or mental. Pain was a part of love.

So, he took another punch to the face.

And another.

And another.

The punches stopped for a moment.

Corey chuckled and spit a wad of blood from his mouth. "Ah, just like old times, Pops."

The fake (but all too familiar) father smiled. As if he was an actor doing his best not to break character, but was secretly enjoying it too much for it to not show. He smiled slightly as he threw down another fist that connected with Corey's jaw.

Corey fell from the chair. He felt the smashed remains of his glasses beside him.

Well, he thought to himself, *at least I won't be able to see myself in the mirror after this one.*

His fake-father threw another punch as Corey brought out his hand, holding a snapped arm from his eye glasses. The stem pierced through his fake-father's fist.

"Fuck!" he yelled as he recoiled his fist. Blood flowed from the wound.

"Hey, look at that," Corey said. "I finally made you bleed."

"Not as much as I'm going to make you," his fake-father said, driving his fist forward.

The stem of the glasses was now nothing more than a sharp object attached to his father's fist. It pierced his chest over and over and over.

Every time it punctured his chest, he heard a wet suction sound.

Corey lost track of the times his father's fist punctured his chest with the stem of the glasses.

The fake-father finally pulled the stem from his fist and turned toward the wall.

"What was the last thing I told your brother before I died?" he asked.

Corey felt weak. Even with the warm blood pooling on his chest, he felt cold.

His fake-father nodded towards the men behind Corey, who smacked him in the back of the head, bringing his attention back to the situation.

"If you want me to let you go, you'll answer me."

Corey tried to talk, but it was difficult. The pain radiated through his entire body. A sharp sting. "Huh?"

"I said, what was the last thing I told your brother before I ate a bullet and painted my brains across our garage door?"

Corey took a couple breaths and prepared himself for talking. "Umm... 'Take–take Co–Corey to sc–chool tomorrow and you'll be home a–after work.'"

The fake-father laughed. "What a weird thing to lie about."

"I kn–know," Corey said.

"You know? You knew that your brother lied to you?"

Corey nodded. "Yeah."

"Why did he lie?" his fake-father asked.

"Because... whatever thing you actually said... he didn't want to give you a chance at redeeming yourself."

The fake version of his father nodded. "I see. That's very clever. Didn't work, did it?"

Corey shook his head.

"Why?"

Corey took a deep breath, "You we–were beyond redeeming. The best thing y–you ever did wi–th your life was creating us. You–you peaked."

The fake-father smiled. "Exactly." He then walked over to the table of moldy cookies and stale coffee. He picked up a cookie and took an exaggerated bite. "Would you like to know what I really said to your brother?"

Corey thought about it for a moment.

He shook his head, "I honestly... couldn't care fucking less... to know what shit he thought was important. So, no."

"Very well," his fake-father snapped his fingers and in one swift motion, every person sitting in the chairs stood up and marched out of the room.

Corey tried to sit up straight as he watched the group open the door and exit the room, leaving only him and his fake-father.

"Your father never really loved you, you know?" he said.

"That's fi–fine. He was a fuck–fucking bitch, so... who cares?" Corey laughed at the idea of saying that to his actual father. Something he sometimes daydreamed about back at home. Watching his father's face in shock as the words left his mouth. However, much like what he just experienced, he was positive it would end with his father beating him to a pulp.

The fake version of his father chuckled and turned towards the table. He grabbed it with both hands and flung it in the air.

Coffee flew from the pot. Moldy cookies soared. Paper plates and napkins followed. And under the table, hidden below the red cloth, was Corey's wife.

"Hali!"

His fake-father stood her up, removed the cloth that was tucked into her mouth, untied her wrists and legs, and let her go.

As if he was deciding what to do next, the man stood there, towering over her. Finally, he patted her on the head and walked out of the room, allowing the door to slam behind him.

Corey moved towards his wife, falling to the ground almost immediately. Corey adjusted his hands and knees, looking up just as Hali arrived at his side. He grabbed her in his arms, holding not just his wife, but onto hope. Hope that things down here could work out. With his wife in his hands (something Corey wasn't positive could happen again), he felt hope. It wasn't going to be easy. Things would probably find a way to get worse, but at the end of it all… Corey knew they had a shot.

"Where is everyone?" Hali asked.

Corey took a deep breath. "I–I don't know."

Hali peeled back. "You lost them?"

Corey shook his head. "We sep–perated."

Hali looked down at his wounds, noticing them for the first time. She pulled up Corey's shirt and inspected the damage to his chest. "Oh, my God, Corey. What happened?" She stood and walked away from him to grab the red tablecloth that had hidden her only moments ago, and came back to apply pressure with it.

Corey shrugged. "Sh–shoulda seen t–he other guy."

"I did see the other guy, Core. He seemed fine," Hali said with a hint of annoyance in her voice. She continued to press the cloth against his chest. "Are you going to be able to walk far?"

Corey closed his eyes and tried to gather the energy. With the help of his wife, he was able to stand. "Yeah, I think I can. It'll just be a little slow."

Hali looked around the room. "I think we should get moving." She helped Corey take a couple steps towards the door and then looked up at her husband. "So, you don't know what happened to James?"

"I–I saw him— get carried away… like y–ou and Robyn," Corey said as he struggled to walk. His shirt was almost entirely red and soaked with blood. He could feel his face swelling from the beating. It felt like the skin would stretch until it snapped. Hali stopped.

"What?" Corey asked.

Hali looked around the room. "I want to show you something."

Corey tried to follow her gaze. "I–I don't–what do you mean?"

Hali helped Corey turn entirely around, pointing him to the opposite side of the room, towards the back exit. "When they first brought me down here, they showed me something interesting I think you should see."

Corey didn't argue. He didn't care to see whatever it was, but he also didn't know if going back the way he came was any better of an idea. There wasn't any guarantee that the support group wasn't waiting outside the door to finish him and her off.

The steps seemed to be more and more painful each time he moved. Corey could see Hali was doing her best to act as a crutch, helping him move less of his weight as they walked, but she was small. Corey didn't know how long she could continue.

"Through here," she said as she walked towards the exit door, peeling back the curtain that hung over it. "Honestly, I think there might be a way out through here. I think that's the reason it was locked when you tried to open it."

Hali carefully released Corey and walked over to the door. She twisted the handle and it opened. The door pushed back and revealed the cave once again. The dim, yellow lights of the room died abruptly in the tunnels of the cave. Like their entire purpose was to kill any light that entered.

"You-you know I tr–ied this door?" Corey asked.

Hali turned around and reached a hand out for Corey. "I figured. I heard you walking around and talking from this direction."

With her help, Corey carefully walked out of the room that felt familiar in an alien way, and stepped into the cold and uninviting tunnels he had spent weeks trying to escape. Corey tried to look up from the ground, to gauge what they were looking for, but it really hurt. The sharp pain in his chest, neck, and face made it very difficult to do anything.

Hali looked at him as she pulled out a small flashlight and shined it into the dark tunnel. "We got this. Let's just take it slow. See that rock over there?" she asked, aiming her light on it.

Corey nodded.

"Let's make it there, and then rest."

Corey nodded again.

They moved slowly through the tunnels. Cold air ripped through the passageways and left a chill on Corey's skin. He felt a rush of energy. There might actually be a way out ahead. The air in the tunnel was usually stale and stiff. Cold air implied that there was some place for air to enter the caves. This is it. They were going to get out. Get help. Rescue everyone.

Corey looked down at his wounds. Would he make it that long?

Hali sat Corey down on the agreed upon rock.

He looked up at her and said, "I might no–t make it."

Hali didn't answer.

"I ne–ed you to go and get us som–e help."

She smiled. The same smile that Corey fell in love with. Her stupid smile had gotten her out of so many fights. Corey didn't care that he was weak around her; he was supposed to be. Everything in life could fall apart around him, but around Hali… he was at home.

"Please," Corey said.

"Do you think you have the energy to see the thing I wanted to show you?" Hali asked as she stood up and reached a hand out to her husband.

Corey took a deep breath and focused. "Yeah," he said. He took Hali's hand and let her help him up.

"It's just around here," she said.

Corey had a hard time focusing on anything but the ground in front of him as they walked. He could feel himself losing it. He was losing too much blood. His body was cold, colder than he had ever been in his life.

"Almost there," Hali said.

Her voice was all Corey had to hold onto. Her soft, familiar voice was so comforting for Corey as they carefully walked through the tunnel. He remembered the first time they talked on the phone. He was caught off guard by how small her voice was. It was so cute that it made falling in love with her so much easier.

"Sit here," Hali said as she helped lower him onto another rock.

"O–kay, now what?"

Hali handed him the little flashlight and walked away.

"Wait," Corey said as he fumbled the flashlight. "Wher–re are y–ou go–going?!" Corey reached down and picked up the flashlight, aiming it down the hallway to find his wife. "Hali?"

He stood, using the rock as leverage to push himself up.

Weakly, he moved forward with the light directed at his feet so that he could watch his steps. He moved slowly, step after step, careful not to fall. He hesitated when he noticed something at the edge of the light. Corey slowly directed the flashlight back the way he came, opposite the side of the rock he'd been resting on.

There was hair. Long, brown hair.

He moved the light all the way back to the source of the hair.

"No," he said as he dropped the light.

Corey fell to the ground and crawled.

He didn't know he had that much energy still as he moved as quickly as possible.

"No, no, no."

Corey positioned the body in his lap and pushed back the hair from its face.

"Hali?" Corey began to cry as he looked down at his wife.

Her body was stiff. She was beaten badly. Her bones in her hands and legs were snapped like twigs. Her skin was white and cold, with the exception of old bruises lining her entire body. They were yellow and purple rings that would not fade. Though her eyes were wide open, a white film was now pulled over them.

She had been dead for a while.

"I d–don't under-stand," Corey said.

"You don't have to," he heard from the dark of the tunnel.

Corey tried to run his hand through his wife's hair, but his fingers got stuck in mats of blood and mud. Tears streamed from his swollen face. "So you–you weren't he–er all this time?"

"Most of it," his wife's voice said from the shadows. "She's been like this since I left her, two weeks or so ago."

Corey pulled her stiff body closer to his own, "Wh–hy did you sh–show me this?" He coughed blood from all the extra energy he was using to talk to her.

"I thought it would be fun," she said.

Corey didn't answer.

With what he had left, he continued to run his hands over his wife's hair. His tears ran down his face and landed on her dead skin.

He didn't look up, otherwise he would have seen the thing-that-looked-like-his-wife sprint out of the shadows towards them.

With a big rock that she slammed into the back of his skull.

Twenty-Two.

Tyler held his wife as they walked down the tunnel.

Away from where his friend had died.

He held his wife in his arms as they moved. He wasn't about to lose her again.

"Hi," James said with an outreached hand.

"Hey, James," Robyn said.

Tyler stopped. "Wait. How did you know his name?"

Robyn looked confused. "What? No, wait, I'm lost."

James looked to Tyler and back to Robyn. "How did you know my name?"

Robyn's eyes squinted as she said, "Because I was with you in Corey's group."

James rocketed forward and grabbed Robyn by her shoulders. "Was Claire there?"

"Yes, she was. And so were you... Have you forgotten everything or something? How did you guys meet?"

"Where is Claire now?" James asked.

Robyn shrugged. "I don't know for sure, but I'm pretty sure she is back at the bottom of the cavern where we left her with Tiff and Doug."

"I've got to go," James said to Tyler.

"I know," Tyler said as they shook hands. "Good luck."

Robyn grabbed Tyler by the collar of his shirt as James sprinted down the tunnel. "If you don't tell me what the fuck is going on, I'm going to punch you in the dick."

"James has been with me. He saved me. He's been separated from his group for a while now," Tyler said.

"Then who have I been with for the last day?" Robyn asked.

"That question is why he is running away from us and towards his wife," Tyler said.

"Wake up," a voice said. "Everything is going to be fine, but you have to wake up."

Claire opened her eyes, slowly at first, but when she registered the voice as coming from her husband, she sprang to life. "Oh, sweet Jesus, James!"

She wrapped her arms around her husband.

"I was so scared," she said. "I had no control over my own body. It was moving without me doing anything, like I was sleepwalking. But I was awake the entire time."

"I know," James said. "I had a helluva time pulling you away. But the further away from the cavern we got, the less you fought. I think we are good now."

"What happened to Tiff and Doug?" she asked.

"I don't know," he said as he let go of Claire. "I think we are alone now. Just us."

"What do we do?" Claire asked.

"I think I have an idea," he said. "You've got to trust me."

"Okay," Claire said as she grabbed her husband's arm. She was gripping him tightly, afraid to let go, but comforted that he was back with her. "I just don't want us to split up again."

Together, they walked down the tunnel.

Claire looked around them. The tunnels were dark, but somewhere at their end was the faint glow of a flame.

"Where are we going?" she asked.

"You've got to trust me," he said. "I can get you out of here."

"Me?" Claire asked. "What do you mean?"

"You are just going to have to go with it," he said. "Okay?"

Claire felt the rush of comfort she'd had holding onto her husband disappear. He felt foreign, distant. She slowly loosened her grip from the vise she had been using before.

Together, they walked down the tunnel.

Claire looked up at her husband and said, "You aren't my husband, are you?"

He didn't look down.

Claire sprang away, running in the opposite direction from the dim light at the end of the tunnel.

"I wouldn't if I were you," he said.

Claire continued to run.

A flashlight shined from over her shoulder, revealing a tall figure further down the tunnel. Its head was bent as if it was too tall to stand fully in the tunnel.

"He won't let you pass," the imposter said.

Claire turned back.

"I don't want to go with you," she said.

"I know," he said. "But this might be the only chance that you and your husband have to get out."

"My husband is still alive then?" Claire asked.

The man that looked like her husband nodded. Even in the low light, she could see the exaggerated movement.

The man held out a hand for hers. "This is the only way."

Claire didn't take his hand, but she did turn back towards the dim light.

"Thatta girl," he said.

They continued down the tunnel side by side. The sound of their footsteps echoing against rock and dirt was all she could hear within the chamber of darkness. She listened for anything else that could give her any indication of what they were walking towards, but there was nothing at all.

As they walked closer to the light, she could see why it was dim. A hoard of cloaked figures obscured it. They lined the walls of the tunnel, pushing as far away as possible, giving Claire and her husband's imposter to walk past.

Claire didn't bother looking at the figures much; they were hardly a shock at this point. Nothing down here shocked her anymore, in fact. She had seen enough bullshit that she felt damaged to her core.

"What happened to everyone else?"

The man looked down at her. "Do you really want to know?"

They continued to walk past the cloaked figures. Though Claire hadn't been counting them, she knew there were easily more than thirty of them already. "I think I do."

He shrugged. "Some of your friends are dead. Others are dying. Some are fine, but don't know they are about to die. Really depends on if you do what I ask you to do."

Finally, they reached the front of the hoard of people. The one standing at the front held a lantern in front of them. It was casting the dim light they'd followed.

"After you," the imposter said, holding his arm out to lead the way.

Claire exited the tunnel and into a small room where there was a rock slab in its center.

"Lay on the table, please," the man said. "This is going to really fucking hurt."

Twenty-Three.

Tiff moved cautiously down the dark tunnel. She wiped stray tears from her eyes as a steady stream continued down her face.

She didn't have any direction to go. No flashlight to lead her.

Tiff just moved as if she knew where she was going. Afraid to stop. Afraid to think about what she was doing and what even a moment of hesitation could cause.

She didn't want to keep going.

She didn't want to fight anymore, but Doug told her she had to.

So, she did.

She had lost hope of finding anyone else alive.

After she left the edge overlooking the dead body of her cousin, she tried looking for Claire. She gave up when she couldn't find her after a couple minutes. James had gotten her first. She wasn't positive why James turned on her and Doug, but she was fairly confident that whatever fate James had in mind for Claire wasn't any better than the fate that had befallen Doug.

Tiff sprinted away from the cavern until she found the familiar dark tunnel that light refused to penetrate. After that, she just kept walking. Walking through one dark tunnel after another.

A blackhole underground.

Tiff let her mind drift to the rest of the party. James was the only one that came back. Was it possible that everyone else was already dead? Was she all that was left of the group? After James finished off Claire, would he kill himself or come after her? Tiff didn't like any of the conclusions her brain reached.

So, she kept moving.

Tiff reached out a hand and ran it along the wall. To her surprise, the jagged edges were no longer there. Instead, the rocks were smooth, almost flat. She could feel them stacked together like bricks. Tiff let her fingers glide up the wall and discovered an arch.

Where was she?

Was this a good sign?

Tiff let her mind wonder. Maybe she was getting closer to an exit. She picked up her pace as her heart began to race with the possibility of breathing fresh air again. Further, she pushed down the rock-bricked tunnel, faster with every step, until she was jogging comfortably through the dark..

Her hands slipped off the wall as it expanded into a larger room. Tiff stopped.

It was still too dark to know where she was, so she blindly waved her hands around until she found the walls of the tunnel again. Feeling the cold and smooth rock beneath her fingers, she used them to lead the way.

Her fingers stopped as the walls turned inwards. She raced her fingers around the edge until she realized she was standing in front of a doorway.

A blinding light suddenly bounced off the walls. Tiff shielded her eyes from the unexpected assault on her eyes. She turned around to face a dark figure, hidden behind a flashlight.

"I wouldn't go through there if I were you," a voice said.

Tiff looked back and saw that she was standing in front of a selection of four doorways. Across the small room, the person with the flashlight leaned against another entrance.

"A couple of those four rooms are going to try and kill you," the person said.

"Who are you?" she asked.

The person lowered their flashlight and aimed it at their face.

"Bird?" Tiff looked at the face of the man she had barely met. It was swollen now, bleeding with chunks of flesh missing. His clothes were shredded and covered in crimson stains.

"Yup," he said with a smile.

Tiff took a step forward, then hesitated. "How do I know this isn't a trap?"

Bird shrugged. "How do I know that *you* aren't a trap?"

The two of them stood quietly, studying one another.

It was true, she didn't know if this was just another trick the cave was throwing at her. She only had two choices. She could blindly trust him, hope that this really was the man she met the day before, or leave and continue without him. Hoping all the while that he didn't follow and attack her whenever her guard dropped. However, she wasn't positive he'd be able to catch her even if he wanted to. He looked hurt. Badly.

"How'd you find this place?" she asked.

"I, uh, I was separated from Robyn. We were attacked by these stupid fucking spiders, and I was overrun. I helped Robyn escape, but knew that I wasn't going to be able to follow her," Bird said. "So, I just ran. I kept running and running. It was pitch dark in the tunnels and I didn't have a flashlight to guide me. Eventually, after what felt like forever, I felt the tunnel changing. I then found this room." Bird pointed behind himself. "Inside, I found some supplies. Some food. A water bottle. And a flashlight."

Tiff leaned over and looked into the room behind him. While scanning the space, she noticed Bird was wearing a backpack.

"Where are you going?" she asked.

Bird unzipped the backpack as he approached her. He pulled out a granola bar and handed it to her. "Eat this and follow me."

Tiff didn't need to be told twice. She ripped open the bar and ate it in one giant bite. She felt crumbs fall from her mouth, which she tried to catch with her hands and eat.

She followed Bird through the third door. The rocky-bricks of the outer room were replaced by ruby and gold bricks. The room was covered entirely in the shockingly out of place bricks. Everywhere except the center of the room.

There was a door made of rock and dirt carved into the furthest wall.

"I found our way out," Bird said.

Tiff reached out and ran her fingertips over the cold door. "Where does it go?"

Bird reached down and opened the door.

On the other side were trees and grass. A rush of cold air swarmed over her with the smell of seawater and pine trees, reminding her of the summers she spent on the Oregon Coast.

"What about your brother and everyone else?" Tiff asked.

Bird's gaze dropped to the ground. Tiff could see he was struggling with the decision he was about to make.

"I'm not in any condition to keep fighting my way through the cave. I–I need to get help for them. I need to heal and come back for them, better prepared."

Tiff took his hand and said, "Okay, then that's what we'll do."

Bird let out a deep breath. "What if what's behind this door is worse than what we are leaving?"

Tiff shrugged. "Then we at least get to see the sun again. Plus, I have a good feeling about this."

She took a step forward, out of the door and onto the soft dirt littered with dead pine needles. Tiff reached back for Bird and said, "We can do this."

Bird looked over his shoulder toward the tunnels as he struggled to make his choice.

"Let's just look around," Tiff suggested.

Bird looked back at her and said, "Okay."

He stepped through the door and closed it behind him.

Unsure of where they were going and where they were, the two entered a forest full of trees.

Twenty-Four.

James ran through the tunnels, checking the ceiling at every corner for the directional arrows to help guide him.

If Claire was back at the cavern, this would be the fastest way to find her.

However, the first couple corners were bare. They either hadn't come this way before, or James was in such a rush that he'd missed them entirely.

A wave of hope rushed through his veins when he finally located an arrow.

"Fuck yes," he said to himself.

He followed the arrow's guidance to another arrow at another corner. James made his turn and flew down the tunnel, his flashlight bouncing off the walls as he sprinted towards his ultimate goal.

Claire.

Claire was all that kept him going all this time.

He was going to find her, *had* to find her.

James sprinted to the next corner, inspected it for another arrow, and followed it accordingly.

He was moving as fast as he possibly could, until something stopped him dead in his tracks.

His flashlight beam suddenly revealed a man standing at the end of the tunnel he was headed to.

James was staring at an identical version of himself.

"Hello," it said.

"Where is Claire?" James yelled.

The copy of himself shrugged. "She's... fine."

"What does that mean?"

"That she's at least alive," it said. "And that's really the best you could ask for."

"Where is she at?"

The man looked behind him, down the tunnel, before turning to his right and walking away.

"Wait!" James screamed as he sprinted towards the corner.

As his flashlight bounced off the walls of the surrounding tunnel, he saw his other version running away.

James checked the arrow atop the corner and realized it was pointed in the opposite direction.

"You won't find her that way," his twin said.

James gritted his teeth and followed him through the labyrinth.

He didn't know where he was going or if he was willingly running toward a trap, but he knew one thing: Whenever he found Claire, he was going to kill this thing that looked like him. He was going to make sure it was nothing more than a pile of mush and blood before he left this place.

As fast as he was able to run, James pushed down the tunnel. No matter how fast he moved, he was unable to catch his duplicate. He was always out of reach.

Still, James followed, thinking he was making the right choice. *Hoping* he was making the right choice.

The tunnel opened.

James froze.

They were out of the tunnels and back in the giant part of the cave they'd crawled into weeks ago. The place where they first met Kami and were tricked into diving further and further into the dark unknown.

James looked around and saw the other version of himself standing thirty yards away, looking back at him. Waiting.

"Almost there," it said.

James didn't run. Something was off.

Why would this twin lead him to the entrance? After everything he had experienced in the cave, this was the most baffling. From what he'd gathered, everything the cave did up until this point was to drive them further and further inside.

He followed his duplicate around the vast room, navigating around the stalagmite that reached higher than James' head. The cave felt different than the tunnels. There was cold air moving throughout the space. It felt damp and empty.

James continued forward until he saw something he hadn't noticed the first time in the cave.

There were two doors, one on each side of the small hole they'd crawled through to enter the cave in the first place.

"She's inside here," his twin said, pointing to the door at its left.

"You're positive?" James asked.

It smiled back at him. "One hundred percent."

"Good," James said as he slowly approached the door. He turned back to the version of himself. "Then I guess we are done here."

"I guess we are," it said back to him.

James balled his hand into a fist, ready to attack.

"Go ahead," it said with a smile. "I know you want to."

James threw a punch into the face of his clone, knocking it backwards. James was quick to capitalize on its fall by jumping on top of it. He threw punch after punch until his fists were raw and bruised. He continued to punch as blood sprung from its face and landed onto James. He then picked it up by the back of the head and began to slam it onto the rocky floor. The *cracking* and *popping* of bones echoed through the cave.

The clone was no longer moving.

James couldn't even recognize its face anymore. He tried his best to gather his breath as he wiped his bloody fists on the shirt of the dead clone.

"James," a female voice said. "If you're done, we are ready."

He turned around and saw Kami standing in the open doorway.

"What the fuck are *you* doing here?" James said as he bounded to his feet. His fists were already raw and hurt beyond reason, but he was ready to keep fighting.

Kami turned to allow another woman to step forward.

"Claire?" James said.

"We are so close, James. We are almost out."

Twenty-Five.

Robyn and Tyler walked hand and hand through the tunnel, a single flashlight source guiding the way as they moved.

Robyn didn't care.

She was slowly coming to the conclusion that they weren't going to make it out alive. They were going to die down here, and her biggest fear was not knowing what happened to Tyler. If she was being honest with herself, she didn't *actually* think Tyler was still alive. Robyn pushed the thought to the deepest part of her brain. Scared at what it meant if she put time into it. The idea of him surviving the night in the dark corners of the cave seemed unrealistic. However, to her surprise, he survived. Here he was. She gripped his hand tighter.

He squeezed hers back.

"We are going to be okay," Tyler said to her.

She didn't believe him. She wasn't even sure if *he* believed himself. Still, it was nice to hear. Robyn just smiled and nodded.

Whatever was coming their way, they would handle it together.

"Remember that Christmas when I bought you that water bottle, blanket, and framed picture?" Tyler said.

She didn't have to think hard about it; she knew exactly what he was talking about. She pulled him closer and wrapped her entire arm around his. "Yeah, I loved that picture."

"I did, too," Tyler chuckled to himself. "Remember what you gave me?"

Robyn smiled. "Yeah, I do."

"The little, red box," Tyler said. "I remember opening it and feeling like an asshole when I saw what was inside."

Robyn laughed. "Why would you?"

"Because, I bought you a couple horror themed nick-nacks and a picture I'd printed from my phone."

"But I love that picture!" Robyn said. "I really do."

"I know you do," Tyler said. "I was just shocked when I opened the box and saw what you had gotten me. You had put so much thought into it."

"I've always been better at gift giving than you," Robyn laughed. "Plus, when I saw it, I knew I needed to buy it for you."

"It's my fav–"

Tyler stopped.

"What?" Robyn felt a jolt of fear rush through her veins. She had gotten so lost in remembering that moment that she'd forgotten they were walking through the tunnels.

She looked ahead of them and saw the tunnel open up, revealing the giant entrance of the cave.

"Wait? How did we get back here?" she asked. "We found it."

Tyler looked down at her. "I don't think we *found* anything."

He moved forward, pulling her along.

"What do you mean?"

"I think the cave is *giving* it to us," he said.

Robyn thought about that for a moment, and realized she had no reason to disagree. She couldn't explain most of the things they had seen down here. Plus, she had no idea what Tyler had seen while they were separated. It was very possible he was right.

"Then why are we walking towards it?" she asked.

Tyler looked down at her as they walked. "What else are we going to do?"

They moved out of the tunnel and into the vast open cave they'd entered in what felt like years ago.

There were the stalagmites standing from the ground for centuries. Giant boulders surrounding the exterior walls. Stalactites hanging from the roof, threatening to snap and dive into them.

Robyn and Tyler moved hand and hand through the cave.

Tyler used the flashlight to guide them around rocks and anything they could trip over. They moved slowly, watching the shadows for anything about to attack.

"There," Tyler said, pointing his flashlight towards a wall twenty yards away.

It was the front of the cave, where they'd climbed through to enter. The tight squeeze had made Robyn feel claustrophobic. She didn't think about it until that moment, but she was going to have to crawl through it all over again.

"What's that?" she asked as they got closer.

There were two doors, one on each side of the hole. And in front of it all, a pool of blood.

"I don't think we were the first one to make it this far," Tyler said.

"What do you think happened?" she asked.

Tyler shrugged.

It didn't matter.

Either they were walking towards the same fate as whoever bled out on the ground in front of the hole, or it wasn't their problem.

Finally, the couple approached the exit.

"You ready?" Tyler asked.

Robyn took a deep breath and prepared to crawl once again. "Yeah."

Tyler handed her the flashlight. "I'll be right behind you."

She hesitated for a moment, then made a move forward.

"I wouldn't do that if I were you," a voice said.

Robyn looked to her right.

The door was open.

Out stepped a man. He was dirty. His clothes hung from his bones like they were his father's and he was just a child. His face had long, scraggly facial hair. The top of his head had a rat's nest of hair. He looked like he had been underground for ages.

"Why not?" Tyler asked.

The man looked over at Tyler and said, "You can, but *she* shouldn't."

Robyn looked up at her husband.

"Come on," the man said. "I'll explain it to you." He turned and walked back inside.

Robyn stood and moved away from the exit, towards her husband.

"What do we do?" she asked.

"I guess we see what he's talking about," Tyler said.

"Why? Why not just go?" Robyn said.

"If I've learned anything about this place, it's that we don't know shit about this place." He took her hand. "Let's see."

Tyler led them through the door. The other side was unlike anything Robyn had seen while below ground. The door led to a small room with smooth walls that looked as if they were carved out of rock. In the center of the room was a table.

An actual table.

It looked foreign in the room.

On one side of the table were two chairs. A third was stationed on the opposite side.

The man took a seat in the lone chair, motioning with his hands for them to join him at the table.

Tyler looked at Robyn. She could see in his eyes that he was both scared and curious. Robyn didn't feel good about it, but trusted her husband.

They sat.

"Well," the man said. "Let's start with introductions. My name is Ben."

The man paused and waited for them.

"Move along," Tyler said.

Ben chuckled. "Fair enough. I remember feeling the same way as you when I was sitting where you are now." He ran his hands through his hair and said, "How about a story?"

Again, he paused, waiting for them to respond.

"Sure," Tyler said. "A story."

Ben smiled. "It's a story that you'll find very familiar." He leaned back in his chair and continued. "Back in 2006, my wife, myself, and a group of our friends found this *hole* in the Linkville tunnels. We saw the challenge."

"The challenge?" Robyn asked.

"For those who seek the light," Tyler said flatly.

Ben pointed to his nose, "Bingo. We saw it and wanted to see what it was about. We climbed in. The hole led us through some bullshit, tight-ass pipe-like tunnels that we eventually managed to crawl through until we were here. Well, not *here*." He pointed out the door. "Out there. In the cave. Anyways, we were tired. Exhausted. We didn't feel right being down here anymore, so we were about to turn back and get out of here, when we heard someone. A man was screaming at the other end of the cave. He was stranded. He introduced himself as Dillon and that his wife was trapped under a rock. He needed our help. This sound familiar?"

"Familiar enough," Robyn said.

"Good. So we followed him. He led us deep into the cave and through a series of tunnels. Eventually—and I'll cut to the chase because you know where this is going—my friends all died. One by one, they all died. Except my wife and I." He gestured at them. "Much like you find yourself.

"As we were trying to escape, we eventually found ourselves back in the cave where it all started. A door that wasn't there when we entered was now beside the hole," Ben said.

"But there are two doors," Robyn said.

"Very observant," Ben said. "Yes, it's true, there are now two doors. Still, let me finish. So, as we were about to leave, the door opened and out stepped who?"

Robyn shrugged.

"Fucking Santa Claus," Tyler said. "We don't know."

"Dillon," Ben said. "Dillon stepped out."

"So, Dillon is behind all of this?" Robyn asked.

"Not exactly," Ben said. "Let me explain to you what he told me. This cave is part of something *bigger*. There is this island. Some evil fucking island out in the middle of nowhere. It is literally hell on earth. It exists to put evil into our world. Doorways from that island lead all over the world. Through those doorways, evil is let into our world. This cave came from one of those doors. It latched onto our world and formed here. The cave itself is evil because of that island."

"So, everything inside this cave came from the island?" Tyler asked.

"Yes and no. Yes, some of the stuff in here has slipped through the door every now and then. However, the majority of the stuff here was created here. The island conjures up whatever you fear. Spiders? Sure, now there are spiders. Are you afraid of your teeth falling out? Sure, now there is a deranged old man who wants to pull the teeth from your face. Most of the things inside here are only here because, at some point, someone was afraid of it and got trapped down here. And now their fear just exists down here."

"I don't fully follow all of this," Robyn said. "But did Dillon explain to you why he brought you down here?"

"He did," Ben said. "He explained to me that this entire thing has been going on for... more than a hundred years. People have been tricked into going deeper into the caves by someone needing help. Once trapped inside, they are slaughtered. You see, the cave needs it to stay alive and powerful. Otherwise, the door to the island would shut and the cave would cease to have any power. So, it kind of forces people to help it."

"And Dillon was helping the cave?" Tyler asked.

"Not willingly. I spent at least a decade hating him. Blaming him for all this, but now... now I understand him. I get why he did what he had to do."

"What did he have to do?" Tyler asked.

"He had a deal offered to him. Trap twenty souls down here, no matter how long it takes, and find a replacement to carry on the tradition. In exchange, he and his wife would be set free at the end," Ben said.

"So, are you the Dillon in this story or…" Robyn started.

"No," Tyler said. "He's Kami's husband."

"Jesus, man," Ben said. "Spot on. You guys are really good at this. Yes, Kami is my wife. You see, I'm not allowed to leave the cave until we've successfully trapped twenty souls here and I find myself a replacement. My loving wife has been doing whatever she can to get people down here. You see, we've finally reached our quota. We've gotten twenty innocent people to die down here. Now, we just need to find our replacement."

"You want us to take over?" Robyn asked.

"Well, yes," Ben said.

"What if we say no?" Tyler said. "What if we just leave? We are right next to the exit."

"That's why the cave has an insurance policy," Ben pointed to Robyn. "What happened to your shoulder?"

Tyler looked over at her. Robyn instinctively moved her hand to her shoulder. She could still feel it. The crawling below her skin. The slugs shifting through her muscle and bone.

"If you were to try and climb out, sure, you'll get out," Ben said, talking directly to Tyler. "But if *she* tried… she'd die. The slugs would poison her. Same way I could never leave." Ben pulled the collar of his shirt aside, revealing a large scar above his chest.

"So, we don't have a choice?" Tyler said.

"Not really," Ben said with a smile. "But don't worry. You'll both be safe down here. The cave won't bother you as long as you are doing what it needs."

"I think we do have a choice," Robyn said.

"Oh, really?" Ben said with a frown. "What's that?"

"We don't do it," Robyn said. "We don't help you or the cave. We aren't going to bring twenty people down here to their death. So, you won't have a replacement, and you'll be trapped down here longer."

"But I will get out," Ben said. "Kami will find us a replacement. If it's not you, it'll be someone else."

"Yeah, but you won't be walking out of here today," Tyler said as he gripped his wife's hand. "And that seems good enough for me."

Ben smiled. "I can't say I'm not disappointed."

Knock, knock, knock.

Robyn and Tyler turned their heads to the door.

"Enter," Ben said.

The door opened, revealing Kami.

"You good in here?" she said.

Ben looked at the couple. "Last chance?"

Robyn looked at her husband. "You can go. I'm okay."

Tyler smiled at her, lifting her hand and kissing it. "Nah, let's ride this one out."

Ben gave them one last chuckle and walked around the table to the front of the room. He grabbed Kami by the hand and together they crawled through the hole.

"Did they…" Robyn hesitated. "Did they just kill themselves?"

"Why would they do this for over twenty years just to climb through the hole, knowing we weren't going to replace them?" Tyler asked.

"I have no idea," Robyn said.

As soon as the words left Robyn's mouth, there was movement outside the door. Her heart seemed to stop.

Claire and James walked through the door.

Claire's face was swollen with tears.

James looked at them both and said, "I'm so sorry."

Then he slammed the door.

"Wait! No!" Tyler screamed as he jumped from his chair towards the door.

Darkness swallowed them as the lock clicked into place.

"We can get out," Robyn said as she blindly tried finding her husband. "We are going to be fine."

"Stop!" Tyler screamed. "Stop acting like that!"

Robyn reeled back. "What? Acting like what?"

"I should have left! I should have gotten out of here while I could! Now, I'm trapped."

"I'm sorry," Robyn said. "I didn't want you to."

"I fucking swear," Tyler said as turned on his flashlight, shining it in his wife's face. He was raising a fist, red with rage. Ready to attack her. He began to punch the door. Over and over. Screaming the entire time. "I'm not going out like this!"

"Tyler," Robyn said. "Why are you doing this?"

He stopped. His eyes grew wide.

Robyn could see something in his eyes she had never seen before. Hatred. Unbridled hatred. Tyler hated her. His face turned red and his eyes squinted. He peered at her, his chest heaving as he began to work himself up. Tyler raised the flashlight over his head, ready to swing it down on his wife.

Robyn covered her face with her arms.

Nothing.

She waited a moment for him to slam the flashlight down on her, after nothing happened she removed her arms and looked at Tyler.

He lowered the flashlight and moved the beam around the room, searching for something.

"Oh, no," he said.

"What?" she said, following the flashlight beam around the room until she was able to see where he settled it.

In the corner of the room, there was a little girl.

No older than eight years, with braided hair that hung over her shoulder in a white and blue checkered dress.

Her eyes were black.

The End?
Wait, There's More!
The Linkville Horror Series by Mike Salt:

Damned to Hell

Rob is a man whose life has spiraled out of control since the death of his teenage son. He spends most of his nights stumbling home from a bar and his days are spent hungover. Desperate to get his life back on track, and ready to move on, he discovers something "evil" with the promise of giving him closure. And now Rob will do whatever it takes to save his son's life.

The Valley

When Conrad and his wife set out to meet their friends for a simple weekend retreat, all they wanted was an easy weekend full of catching up and drinking. But when the group discovers a map that shows them the location of a hidden waterfall, hidden in the heart of an uncharted valley, they can't help but jump at the opportunity to rediscover it.

What they don't expect is to find an abandoned ghost town. Hidden away from the world with an evil secret.

Now Conrad and his group must do whatever they can to stay alive as they are hunted by an entity that feeds off the horrors that occur in the valley.

A horror they are doomed to repeat for eternity.

The House on Harlan

When reluctant sellout Alex and his family move to Harlan Drive, they soon discover that their idyllic suburban house is not the safe haven it first seems. In fact, there's nothing safe about The House On Harlan at all…

In this thrilling new novella from Mike Salt, author of The Valley and Damned to Hell, you are invited to step inside the House on Harlan – a house where the things that go bump in the night come out in force. A house that is hungry for blood. A house that will haunt you.

A house with a little black door in the cellar…

A door that opens both ways. And, as Alex is about to find out, the things that come through aren't all there is to fear in this house. No, the real danger is waiting for him on the other side…

AVAILABLE EVERYWHERE BOOKS ARE SOLD!

Afterthought

I didn't know when I was writing this story that I was going to focus so much on parental damage. I need and want to acknowledge that this wasn't a reflection on any relationship that is in this book. I personally knew Corey's father growing up and he was one of the strongest, loving, supportive fathers I've ever known. The fictional version of Corey's father is just that—a work of fiction and not at all based on Greg.

The same goes for Bird's father. Bird is based on my brother-in-law, Tyler. I never had the honor of knowing you and my wife's father, but from what I understand he was an amazing father and did nothing but love his children.

Acknowledgments

I would like to thank some people for making this book happen, in no particular order. I'm very sorry if I've left anyone out that belongs in this section of the book.

First, and always first, thank you to my wife, Brianna. You give me so much motivation and drive to keep pushing. You always have an ear ready to listen and walk me through the dead ends I find myself in. I would never have finished any of my books if it wasn't for your support, and for that I'm so grateful. To my kids, the entire group of offspring that live with me: Justin, Kyla, Lennox, and Roswell. I hope you read this one day and see that anything is possible if you really want to accomplish it. Set your goals and go for it. I love you all and am so thankful to have you guys interrupting me every couple minutes as I try to finish my work.

Secondly, I wanted to thank the actual Robyn and Tyler of whom were the inspiration for the main characters in this story. I have always felt so much support from you guys. I really wanted to make you guys the villains in this story, but it just didn't happen. I can't thank you enough for being such great friends that feel like family, and for being an aunt and uncle for our kids. The relationship that you two have with our kids is so important to them and I will always be grateful for your influence on them.

Thank you to the actual Corey, and Hali. Corey, you have been a friend since we were dumb kids doing power-bombs on the trampoline at your house. You've always been one of my closest friends and I'm so thankful to have you in my life. I hope you and your awesome wife, Hali, enjoyed this alternate version of you. I know that *technically* Hali wasn't in the book until she was found dead, but... you know... her evil clone was.

Thank you to a certain group of friends that meet up at our house once a week. You guys deserve to be characters in a later book, and no doubt I'll find the right one to put you in. I am so thankful for all the support you guys have shown me through the years. I truly have found brothers and sisters in this group. I look forward to our trip to the tap house to keep up with traditions of finishing a book.

Thank you to all my spooky friends on IG. This small group of indie horror authors have become more than a group of strangers that share the interest of writing. You guys have made me feel at home and the support I get from the spooky friends have been so instrumental in pulling me out of some very depressing places when I fall behind on my writing. I hope I can return the favor to all of you some day.

To the actual Tyler (or T-bird or just Bird), you have become a brother to me and I am so thankful to have you in my life and an uncle for my children. I hope to help you along your own journey as you try finishing your own book.

And finally, thank you to Andrew Robert and anyone that believed in my work with DarkLit Press. I am so honored and thrilled to be a part of such an impressive catalog of horror work. Thank you to my editor, Aiden Merchant, for making the book less of a mess and actually readable. I promise to learn the English language better for the next book, and make your job a little bit easier. And thank you to Kristina Osborn (Truborn Design instagram: @nw.reader) for the awesome covers. I love all of your work and am so happy that you have jumped on board with the series.

A Note From DarkLit Press

All of us at DarkLit Press want to thank you for taking the time to read this book. Words cannot describe how grateful we are knowing that you spent your valuable time and hard-earned money on our publication. We appreciate any and all feedback from readers, good or bad. Reviews are extremely helpful for indie authors and small businesses (like us). We hope you'll take a moment to share your thoughts on Goodreads and/or BookBub.

You can also find us on all the major social platforms including Facebook, Instagram, and Twitter. Our horror community newsletter comes jam-packed with giveaways, free or deeply discounted books, deals on apparel, writing opportunities, and insights from genre enthusiasts.

VISIT OUR LITTLE-FREE-LIBRARY OF HORRORS!

About the Author

Mike Salt is the author of several horror novels, including *Damned to Hell*, *The Valley*, *House on Harlan*, *Price Manor: The House That Burns*, and this thing you just read. Mike is a lone soldier from the future sent back to stop the apocalypse. However, he's discovered that living in the past is better. He never had nachos before this, and now he can have them whenever he wants. Have you ever had nachos? Like not even fancy ones, Mike gets excited about gas station nachos. The kind that you need to open a small bag and push a button on a dispenser for some warm cheese. He isn't picky. Nachos are pretty fucking good. He's decided to stay and forget about his mission. Now, he writes books to deal with the guilt he has for not saving the world. However, he will never write enough books to forget the betrayal he has done… but he will always have nachos.

Content Warnings

Blood

Violence

Abduction

Murder

Spiders

Tight spaces

Slugs

Tension breaking jokes

Trypophobia

Dead bodies

Heights

Odontophobia (fear of teeth falling out)

DARKLIT
PRESS

Twenty-Six.

Stone clutched his steaming mug of coffee, its comforting warmth a feeble defense against the chilling air that permeated the dimly lit basement of the secluded cabin. The years had passed, but the basement remained frozen in time, untouched by the passage of seasons. Stone had never felt the need to alter its somber atmosphere, as if preserving the stagnant memories of when he and his closest companions had first rented the cabin all those years ago.

It was a place haunted by the spectral echo of Patrick's meticulous arrangements, ensuring everything was in order before vanishing into the enigmatic mist that shrouded the valley. He had left the money needed to purchase the cabin and all the information in a backpack outside the fog. Stone had found it after he passed through the waterfall and left the haunted ghost-town that was Freedom, home of Dixon Davis. The man who slammed an ax upon the sleeping occupants of the small town.

Within these walls, Stone had raised his late wife, Becca, and his two children, yet the cabin never truly embraced them as its own. It clung to an elusive sense of anticipation, as if it awaited the unfolding of a predestined sequence of events. Stone knew that the cabin was his starting point, but didn't know what the next steps would be. For twelve long years, Stone had fervently dedicated himself to unraveling the secrets hidden within the valley. Countless nights were spent poring over faded newspaper clippings, meticulously curated blogs that he had printed from the depths of the web, and the eerie remnants of forgotten lives dictated in diaries and journals discovered in estate sales after inexplicable demises. Each find, no matter how trivial, fueled Stone's desperate search for connections, a haphazard attempt to piece together the elusive truth that lurked just beyond his grasp.

In this relentless pursuit, Stone felt like a solitary wanderer, blindfolded and stumbling through a veiled realm, groping for fragments that might illuminate the darkness. Every corner of the world became a potential clue, every faded diary or crumpled note a flicker of hope in the dim recesses of his mind. But as the years passed and the stack of documents grew, a realization settled deep within Stone's soul—he might never fully understand what happened to his wife and their friends. The pieces remained scattered, the puzzle unresolved, its significance etching a heavy burden upon his shoulders.

As Stone took a contemplative sip from his mug, the bitter taste mingled with a sense of resignation. The cabin whispered hauntingly in the stillness. It was as if the cabin itself held the answers, locked away within its walls, and Stone was merely a hapless puppet caught in its game. Yet, he couldn't tear himself away. The compulsion to seek understanding, to unmask the truth, consumed him, pushing him further down the labyrinthine path of uncertainty.

It was the twenty-fifth anniversary of the vanishing of Burt Hawkins that finally started to put the pieces together. During a fateful camping trip, Burt had gone missing, leaving his three children and their two cousins alone and waiting for him to return. As he read about an annual charity event that was created in his honor, a long-forgotten conversation resurfaced in Stone's mind. In the depths of his memory, he recalled Bryant and Conrad's conversation about that very incident. That Conrad was there when Burt went missing. He was one of the children left behind. The gears of realization turned within Stone's mind, igniting a spark of intrigue that couldn't be dismissed as mere coincidence. With a sense of purpose, he packed his bag for the weekend, entrusting his eldest daughter, Amy, with the responsibility of the trail, and embarked on his journey to the annual charity event held in the mysterious town of Linkville.

It was at this gathering that Stone found himself face to face with Burt Hawkins' offspring—the three children who had been left behind in the desolate campsite all those years ago, along with Conrad and another acquaintance. The passing of time had transformed these once-innocent children into adults, driven by an unyielding determination to uncover the truth surrounding their father's disappearance. A drive that Stone could relate to too much. Each year, like clockwork, they embarked on a somber pilgrimage, combing through the wilderness in search of any signs, any elusive trace that might shed light on the fate of their father. As they shared their painstakingly mapped-out sectors of exploration with Stone, revealing the vast expanse of their years of work, he found himself irresistibly drawn into their haunting narrative.

Eager to unravel the mysteries that lay concealed within the confines of this eerie tale, Stone absorbed every morsel of information, diligently cataloging the arduous hours the children had devoted to their relentless pursuit. After hours of listening and several beers in his belly, he bid them farewell, as they left to get some sleep before they were to head out on their search the next morning.

Stone went home and began to catalog his findings. Trying to find at what point they intersected and connected to the valley.

That was until he turned on the news.

Reports of the kids never returning from their journey.

Days turned into weeks, and they never turned up. As the news of their inexplicable disappearance reverberated throughout the small town of Linkville, a chilling sequel to the disappearance of Burt all those years ago, Stone knew it was only a matter of time that the world forgot about the kids and moved on.

Stone's mind raced, a whirlwind of thoughts and unanswered questions. Memories of the unexplored regions on their meticulously marked map flooded his thoughts. Stone acquired his own map, tracing the remnants of the children's intended path from memory, marking the uncharted territories left untouched in their relentless pursuit of their father's truth.

Two days passed before Stone heard a knock on the cabin door.

Stone cautiously opened the door, revealing a stranger he had never encountered before—Jed. Initial impressions suggested Jed to be a lost hiker, a mere wanderer in search of his bearings. Stone instinctively prepared to redirect him back towards civilization, but before he could utter a single word, Jed stopped him.

"There's something out there," Jed declared, his finger pointing ominously into the depths of the foreboding forest. "You know it. I know it."

A surge of skepticism tinged Stone's response as he vehemently denied any inkling of such a presence. It wasn't uncommon for some nut-job to wander up to the cabin with some crack-pot theories on what happened to him, his wife, and their friends all those years ago.

Yet, Jed, determined to unveil a hidden truth, extended his phone, offering Stone an article detailing the inexplicable disappearance of hikers. The same hikers that Stone had been researching for the past couple days. Jed pulled the phone back, swiped to another article and handed it back to Stone. An article written over a decade ago, about his own hike and losses.

"I know why they never found your friends," Jed said, his voice resonating with an air of certainty.

"Why is that?" Stone asked as he handed the phone back.

"You didn't point them in the right direction. You sent them off somewhere you knew they wouldn't be found. Away from Freedom, the little town in the middle of a valley," Jed said.

Stone looked Jed up and down, "Enlighten me on why you think that."

Jed entered the cabin and removed notebook after notebook of secrets and cryptic clues. Jed unraveled the tapestry of enigmas that enshrouded their lives. He spoke of the elusive doors that bridged dimensions, the existence of a sinister island harboring ancient evils that seeped into the very fabric of reality. Together, over several months, they meticulously connected the elusive dots that had eluded Stone during his solitary quest, piecing together a cohesive plan to confront the malevolence that awaited them.

A plan that they were about to embark on.

Recruit.

Find the island.

And destroy it.